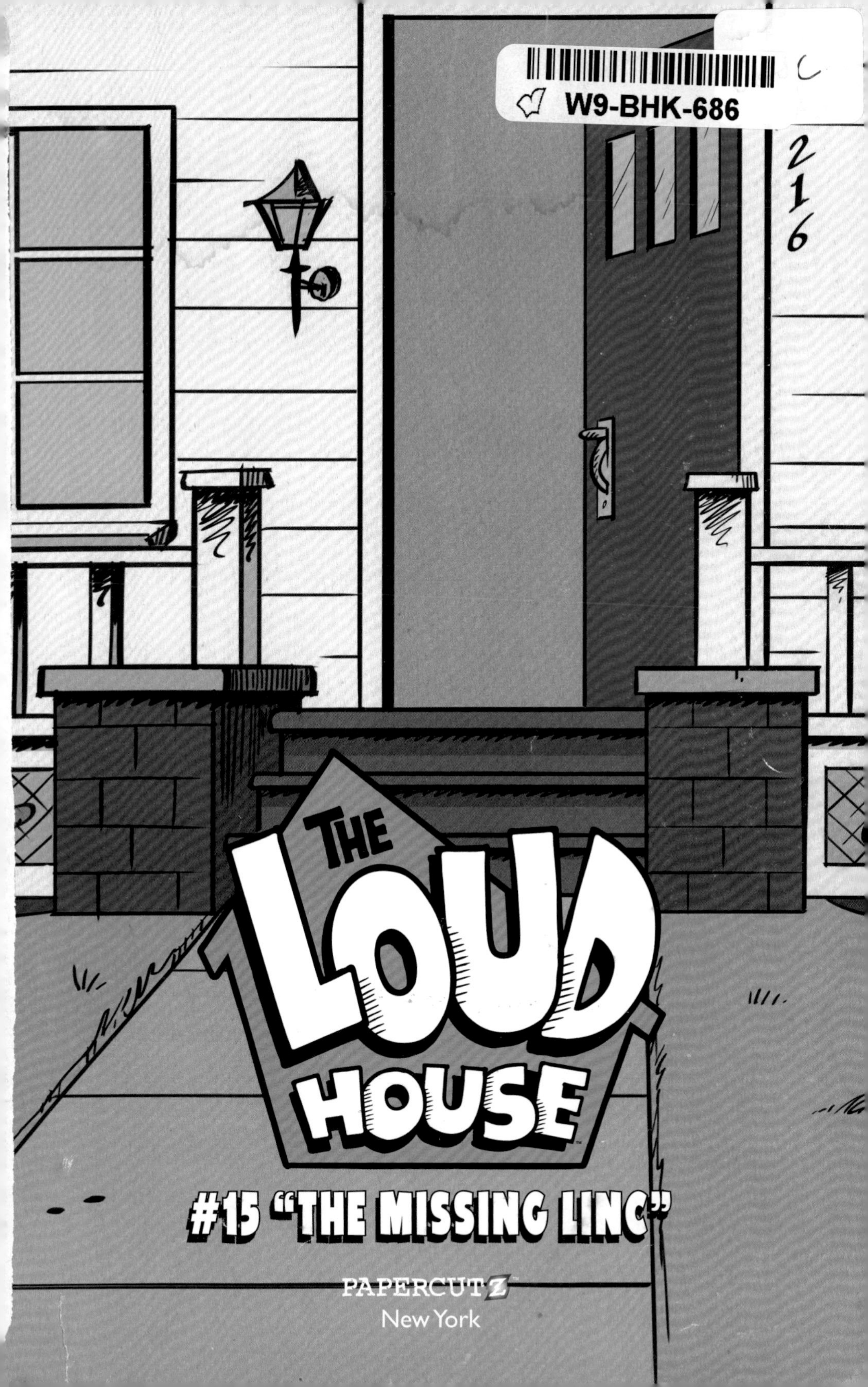
216

THE LOUD HOUSE

#15 "THE MISSING LINC"

PAPERCUTZ
New York

MORE GREAT GRAPHIC NOVEL SERIES AVAILABLE FROM
PAPERCUTZ™

THE SMURFS TALES

BRINA THE CAT

CAT & CAT

THE SISTERS

ATTACK OF THE STUFF

LOLA'S SUPER CLUB

SCHOOL FOR EXTRATERRESTRIAL GIRLS

GERONIMO STILTON REPORTER

THE MYTHICS

GUMBY

MELOWY

BLUEBEARD

GILLBERT

ASTERIX

FUZZY BASEBALL

THE CASAGRANDES

THE LOUD HOUSE

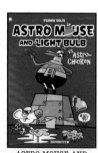
ASTRO MOUSE AND LIGHT BULB

GEEKY F@B 5

THE ONLY LIVING GIRL

papercutz.com
Also available where ebooks are sold.

Melowy, Geronimo Stilton; © 2018 Atlantyca S.pA; The Sisters, Cat & Cat © 2018 BAMBOO ÉDITION; Brina the Cat © 2021 TUNUÉ (Tunué s.r.l.); Attack of the Stuff © 2021 Jim Benton; Lola's Super Club © Christine Beigel + Pierre Fouillet, 2010, Bang. Ediciones, 2011, 2013; School for Extraterrestrial Girls © 2021 Jeremy Whitley and Jamie Noguchi; Mythics © 2021 Éditions Delcourt; GUMBY ©2018 Prema Toy Co., Inc.; Bluebeard © 2018 Metaphrog; Gillbert © 2021 Art Baltazar; ASTERIX® -OBELIX® -IDEFIX® -DOGMATIX® © 2021 HACHETTE LIVRE; Fuzzy Baseball © 2018 by John Steven Gurney; The Loud House and The Casagrandes © 2018 Viacom International Inc.; Manosaurs © 2018 Stuart Fischer and Papercutz; Geeky Fab Five ©2021 Geeky Fab Five LLC.; The Only Living Girl © 2018-2019 Bottled Lightening LLC.

THE LOUD HOUSE

#15 "THE MISSING LINC"

nickelodeon THE LOUD HOUSE #15 "THE MISSING LINC"

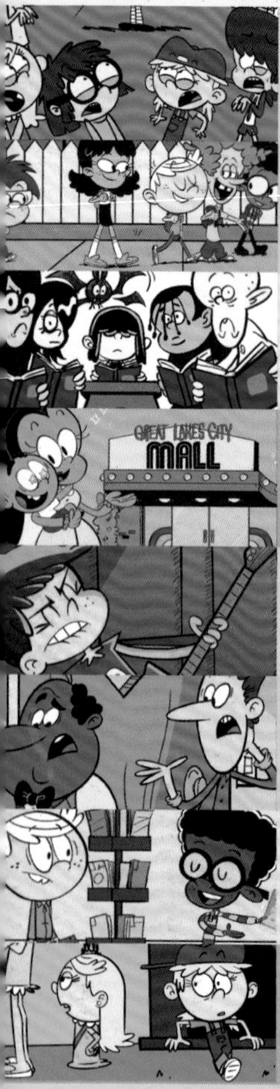

GREAT LAKES CITY
MALL

"THE MISSING LINC"
Caitlin Fein— Writer
Amanda Tran — Artist, Colorist
Wilson Ramos Jr. — Letterer

"A DIRTY RESCUE"
Kacey Huang-Wooley— Writer
Amanda Lioi — Artist
Erin Rodriguez — Colorist
Wilson Ramos Jr. — Letterer

"I BELIEVE"
Kevin Cannarile— Writer
DK Terrell — Artist, Colorist
Wilson Ramos Jr. — Letterer

"FAN FRENZY"
Jair Holguin — Writer
Joel Zamudio — Artist, Colorist
Wilson Ramos Jr. — Letterer

"AN UNDEAD DEBATE"
Kacey Huang-Wooley— Writer
Kiernan Sjursen-Lien — Artist, Colorist
Wilson Ramos Jr. — Letterer

"LISA'S PAPER VIEW"
Kacey Huang-Wooley— Writer
Kelsey Wooley — Artist, Colorist
Wilson Ramos Jr. — Letterer

"MALL TRIP"
Paloma Uribe — Writer
Erin Hyde — Artist, Colorist
Wilson Ramos Jr. — Letterer

"CLOSING MIME"
Amanda Fein — Writer
Erin Hyde — Artist, Colorist
Wilson Ramos Jr. — Letterer

"PLAYING TO THE CROWD"
Derek Fridolfs— Writer
Marc Stone — Artist
Erin Rodriguez — Colorist
Wilson Ramos Jr. — Letterer

"GONE GNOME"
Jair Holguin— Writer
Jessica Gallaher — Artist
Erin Rodriguez — Colorist
Wilson Ramos Jr. — Letterer

"CONSTRUCTION CONUNDRUM"
Kiernan Sjursen-Lien — Writer
Joel Zamudio — Artist, Colorist
Wilson Ramos Jr. — Letterer

"FRIENDS FUR-EVER"
Caitlin Fein— Writer
DK Terrell — Artist, Colorist
Wilson Ramos Jr. — Letterer

"THE TEAM UP"
Derek Fridolfs— Writer
Ron Bradley — Artist, Colorist
Wilson Ramos Jr. — Letterer

"PURRSONAL HYGIENE"
Kiernan Sjursen-Lien — Writer, Artist, Colorist
Wilson Ramos Jr. — Letterer

"SISTER NATURE"
Derek Fridolfs— Writer
Angela Zhang — Artist
Erin Rodriguez — Colorist
Wilson Ramos Jr. — Letterer

"ONE GOOD PUSH"
Kevin Cannarile— Writer
Lex Hobson — Artist, Colorist
Wilson Ramos Jr. — Letterer

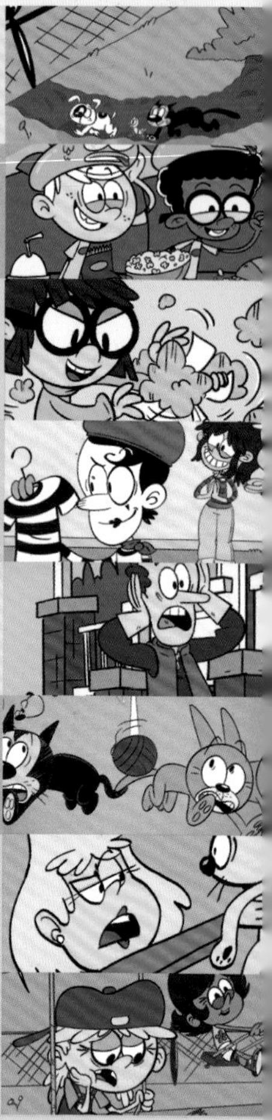

ERIN HYDE — Cover Artist
JORDAN ROSATO — Endpapers
JAMES SALERNO — Sr. Art Director/Nickelodeon
JAYJAY JACKSON — Design
EMMA BONE, CAITLIN FEIN, KRISTEN G. SMITH, NEIL WADE, DANA CLUVERIUS, MOLLIE FREILICH, KRISTEN YU-UM, EMILIE CRUZ, and MICOL HIATT — Special Thanks
JORDAN HILLMAN — Editorial Intern
JEFF WHITMAN — Editor
JOAN HILTY — Editor/Nickelodeon
ARTHUR "DJ" DESIN — Comics Coordinator/Nickelodeon
JIM SALICRUP
Editor-in-Chief

ISBN: 978-1-5458-0868-9 paperback edition
ISBN: 978-1-5458-0867-2 hardcover edition

www.papercutz.com

Papercutz books may be purchased for business or promotional use. For information on bulk purchases please contact Macmillan Corporate and Premium Sales Department at (800) 221-7945 x5442.

Printed in Turkey
March 2022

Distributed by Macmillan
First Printing

MEET THE LOUD FAMILY
and friends!

LINCOLN LOUD
THE MIDDLE CHILD

Lincoln is the middle child, with five older sisters and five younger sisters. He has learned that surviving the Loud household means staying a step ahead. He's the man with a plan, always coming up with a way to get what he wants or deal with a problem, even if things inevitably go wrong. Being the only boy comes with some perks. Lincoln gets his own room — even if it's just a converted linen closet. On the other hand, being the only boy also means he sometimes gets a little too much attention from his sisters. They mother him, tease him, and use him as the occasional lab rat or fashion show participant. Lincoln's sisters may drive him crazy, but he loves them and is always willing to help out if they need him.

LORI LOUD
THE OLDEST

As the first-born child of the Loud Clan, Lori sees herself as the boss of all her siblings. She feels she's paved the way for them and deserves extra respect. Her signature traits are rolling her eyes, texting her boyfriend, Bobby, and literally saying "literally" all the time. Because she's the oldest and most experienced sibling, Lori can be a great ally, so it pays to stay on her good side, especially since she can drive.

LENI LOUD
THE FASHIONISTA

Leni spends most of her time designing outfits and accessorizing. She always falls for Luan's pranks, and sometimes walks into walls when she's talking (she's not great at doing two things at once). Leni might be flighty, but she's the sweetest of the Loud siblings and truly has a heart of gold (even though she's pretty sure it's a heart of blood).

LUNA LOUD
THE ROCK STAR

Luna is loud, boisterous, freewheeling, and her energy is always cranked to 11. She thinks about music so much that she even talks in song lyrics. On the off-chance she doesn't have her guitar with her, everything can and will be turned into a musical instrument. You can always count on Luna to help out, and she'll do most anything you ask, as long as you're okay with her supplying a rocking guitar accompaniment.

LUAN LOUD
THE JOKESTER

Luan's a standup comedienne who provides a non-stop barrage of silly puns. She's big on prop comedy too – squirting flowers and whoopee cushions – so you have to be on your toes whenever she's around. She loves to pull pranks and is a really good ventriloquist – she is often found doing bits with her dummy, Mr. Coconuts. Luan never lets anything get her down; to her, laughter IS the best medicine.

LYNN LOUD
THE ATHLETE

Lynn is athletic and full of energy and is always looking for a teammate. With her, it's all sports all the time. She'll turn anything into a sport. Putting away eggs? Jump shot! Score! Cleaning up the eggs? Slap shot! Score! Lynn is very competitive, but despite her competitive nature, she always tries to just have a good time.

LUCY LOUD
THE EMO

You can always count on Lucy to give the morbid point of view in any given situation. She is obsessed with all things spooky and dark – funerals, vampires, séances, and the like. She wears mostly black and writes moody poetry. She's usually quiet and keeps to herself. Lucy has a way of mysteriously appearing out of nowhere, and try as they might, her siblings never get used to this.

LOLA LOUD
THE BEAUTY QUEEN)

Lola could not be more different from her twin sister, Lana. She's a pageant powerhouse whose interests include glitter, photo shoots, and her own beautiful, beautiful face. But don't let her cute, gap-toothed smile fool you; underneath all the sugar and spice lurks a Machiavellian mastermind. Whatever Lola wants, Lola gets – or else. She's the eyes and ears of the household and never resists an opportunity to tattle on troublemakers. But if you stay on Lola's good side, you've got yourself a fierce ally – and a lifetime supply of free makeovers.

LANA LOUD
THE TOMBOY

Lana is the rough-and-tumble sparkplug counterpart to her twin sister, Lola. She's all about reptiles, mud pies, and muffler repair. She's the resident Ms. Fix-it and is always ready to lend a hand – the dirtier the job, the better. Need your toilet unclogged? Snake fed? Back-zit popped? Lana's your gal. All she asks in return is a little A-B-C gum, or a handful of kibble (she often sneaks it from the dog bowl).

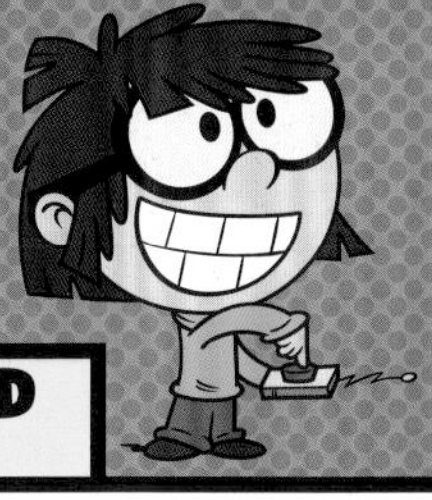

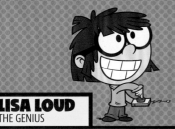

LISA LOUD
THE GENIUS

Lisa is smarter than the rest of her siblings combined. She'll most likely be a rocket scientist, or a brain surgeon, or an evil genius who takes over the world. Lisa spends most of her time working in her lab (the family has gotten used to the explosions), and says her research leaves little time for frivolous human pursuits like "playing" or "getting haircuts." That said, she's always there to help with a homework question, or to explain why the sky is blue, or to point out the structural flaws in someone's pillow fort. Lisa says it's the least she can do for her favorite test subjects, er, siblings.

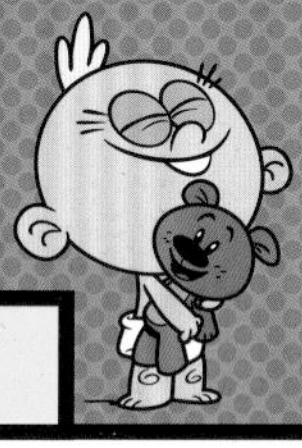

LILY LOUD
THE BABY

Lily is a giggly, drooly, diaper-ditching free spirit, affectionately known as "the poop machine." You can't keep a nappy on this kid – she's like a teething Houdini. But even when Lily's running wild, dropping rancid diaper bombs, or drooling all over the remote, she always brings a smile to everyone's face (and a clothespin to their nose). Lily is everyone's favorite little buddy, and the whole family loves her unconditionally.

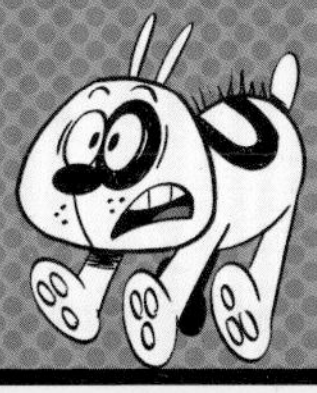

CHARLES

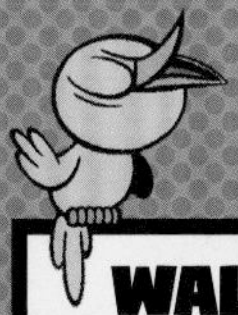

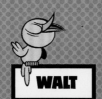

WALT

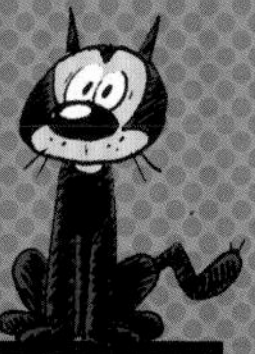

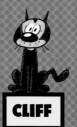

CLIFF

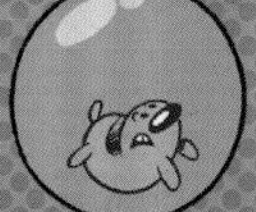

GEO

RITA LOUD

Mother to the eleven Loud kids, Mom (Rita Loud) wears many different hats. She's a chauffeur, homework-checker and barf-cleaner-upper all rolled into one. She's always there for her kids and ready to jump into action during a crisis, whether it's a fight between the twins or Leni's missing shoe. When she's not chasing the kids around or at her day job as a dental hygienist, Mom pursues her passion: writing. She also loves taking on house projects and is very handy with tools (guess that's where Lana gets it from). Between writing, working and being a mom, her days are always hectic but she wouldn't have it any other way.

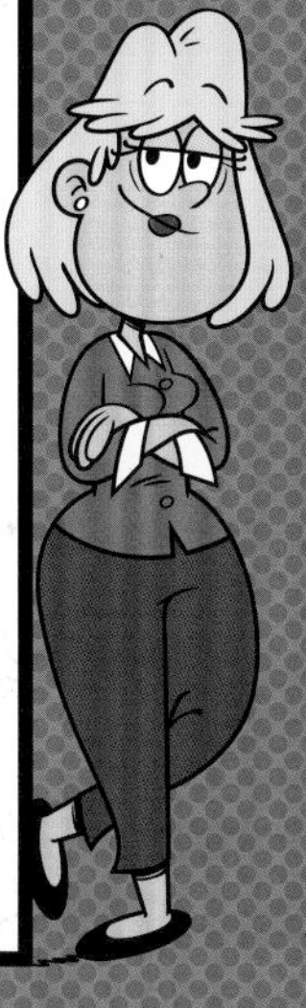

LYNN LOUD SR.

Dad (Lynn Loud Sr.) is a fun-loving, upbeat aspiring chef. A kid-at-heart, he's not above taking part in the kids' zany schemes. In addition to cooking, Dad loves his van, playing the cowbell and making puns. Before meeting Mom, Dad spent a semester in England and has been obsessed with British culture ever since – and sometimes "accidentally" slips into a British accent. When Dad's not wrangling the kids, he's pursuing his dream of opening his own restaurant where he hopes to make his "Lynn-sagnas" world-famous.

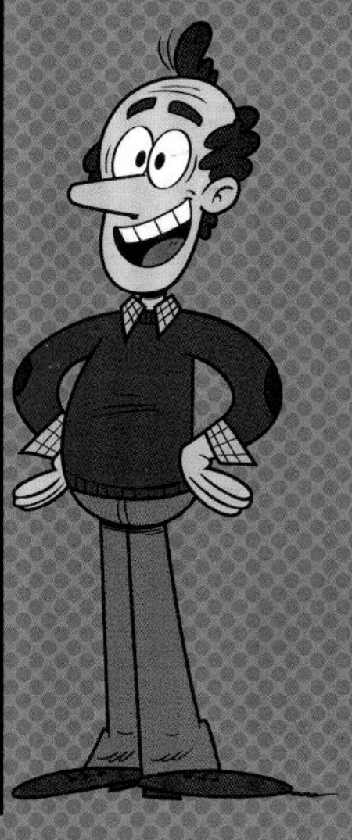

CLYDE McBRIDE
THE BEST FRIEND

Clyde is Lincoln's partner in crime. He's always willing to go along with Lincoln's crazy schemes (even if he sees the flaws in them up-front). Lincoln and Clyde are two peas in a pod and share pretty much all of the same tastes in movies, comics, TV shows, toys—you name it. As an only child, Clyde envies Lincoln—how cool would it be to always have siblings around to talk to? But since Clyde spends so much time at the Loud household, he's almost an honorary sibling anyway.

HAROLD AND HOWARD McBRIDE
Clyde's Loving Dads

Harold and Howard are Clyde's loving dads and only want the best for him, but what they define as "the best" may differ. Harold is a level-headed, straight-shooter with a heart of gold. The more easygoing of Clyde's dads, Harold often has to convince Howard that it's okay for them to not constantly hover over Clyde. Howard is an anxious helicopter parent and it's easy for him to break down into emotional sobbing, whether it be sad times (like when Clyde stubbed his toe) or happy (like when Clyde and Lincoln beat that really tough video game boss). Despite their differing parenting styles, the two dads bring nothing but love to the table.

CLEOPAWTRA
Clyde's Cat

NEPURRTITI
Clyde's Other Cat

POP POP

Albert, the Loud kids' grandfather, currently lives at Sunset Canyon Retirement Community after dedicating his life to working in the military. Pop Pop spends his days dominating at shuffleboard, eating pudding, and going on adventures with his pals Bernie, Scoots, and Seymour and his girlfriend, Myrtle. Pop Pop is upbeat, fun-loving, and cherishes spending time with his grandchildren.

MYRTLE

Myrtle, or Gran-Gran, is Albert's (Pop Pop's) girlfriend. She loves traveling and hanging out with Albert and the Loud kids. Since she doesn't have grandkids of her own, she's the Loud kids' honorary grandma and can't help but smother them with love.

RUSTY SPOKES

Rusty is a self-proclaimed ladies' man who's always the first to dish out girl advice—even though he's never been on an actual date. His dad owns a suit rental service, so occasionally Rusty can hook the gang up with some dapper duds—just as long as no one gets anything dirty.

LIAM HUNNICUTT

Liam is an enthusiastic, sweet-natured farm boy full of down-home wisdom. He loves hanging out with his Mee Maw, wrestling his prize pig Virginia, and sharing his farm-to-table produce with the rest of the gang.

STELLA ZHAU

Stella, is a quirky, carefree girl who's new to Royal Woods. She has tons of interests, like trying on wigs, playing laser tag, eating curly fries, and hanging with her friends. But what she loves the most is tech — she always wants to dismantle electronics and put them back together again.

ZACH GURDLE

Zach is a self-admitted nerd who's obsessed with aliens and conspiracy theories. He lives between a freeway and a circus, so the chaos of the Loud House doesn't faze him. He and Rusty occasionally butt heads, but deep down, it's all love.

CARLOTA CASAGRANDE

Carlota is CJ, Carl, and Carlitos' older sister. A social media influencer, she's excited to be like a big sister to Ronnie Anne. She's a force to be reckoned with, and is always trying to share her distinctive vintage style tips with Ronnie Anne.

CARLITOS CASAGRANDE

The redheaded toddler who is always mimicking everyone's behavior, even the dog's. He's playful, rambunctious, and loves to play with the family pets.

MR. BUD GROUSE

Mr. Grouse is the Louds's next-door-neighbor. The Louds often go to him for favors which he normally rejects – unless there's a chance for him to score one of Dad's famous Lynn-sagnas. Mr. Grouse loves gardening, relaxing in his recliner and keeping anything of the Louds's that flies into his yard (his catchphrase, after all, is "my yard, my property!").

FIONA

Fiona works at Reininger's department store and is also one of Leni's best friends. Fiona is strong and snarky; her sense of humor is much dryer than the others'. She has little patience for people wasting her time – when it comes to Fiona, you need to get right to the point.

HAIKU	MORPHEUS	PERSEPHONE	DANTE	BERTRAND	BORIS

MORTICIANS CLUB

"THE MISSING LINC"

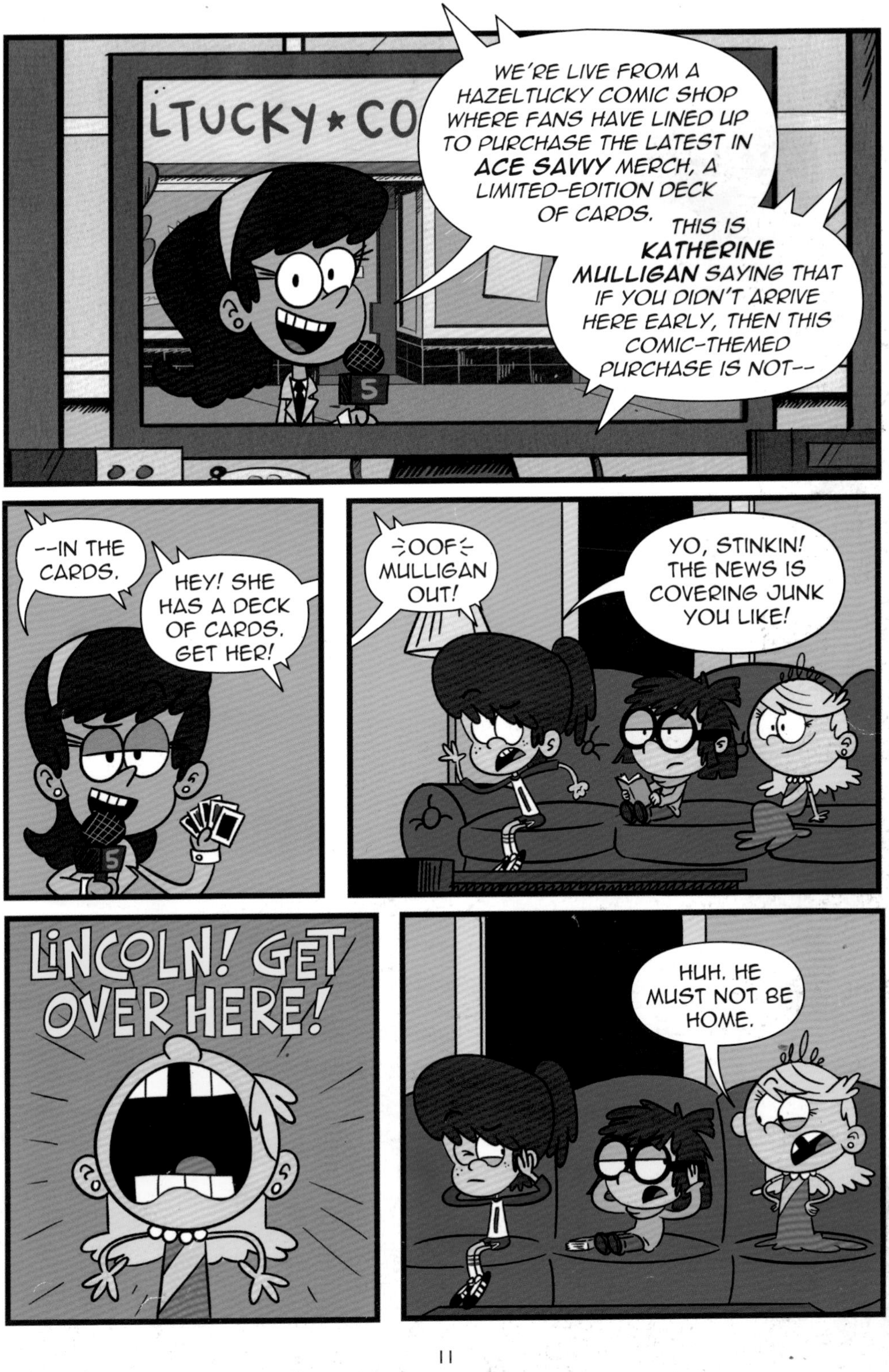
LTUCKY ★ CO
WE'RE LIVE FROM A HAZELTUCKY COMIC SHOP WHERE FANS HAVE LINED UP TO PURCHASE THE LATEST IN ACE SAVVY MERCH, A LIMITED-EDITION DECK OF CARDS.
THIS IS KATHERINE MULLIGAN SAYING THAT IF YOU DIDN'T ARRIVE HERE EARLY, THEN THIS COMIC-THEMED PURCHASE IS NOT--
--IN THE CARDS.
HEY! SHE HAS A DECK OF CARDS. GET HER!
OOF MULLIGAN OUT!
YO, STINKIN! THE NEWS IS COVERING JUNK YOU LIKE!
LINCOLN! GET OVER HERE!
HUH. HE MUST NOT BE HOME.

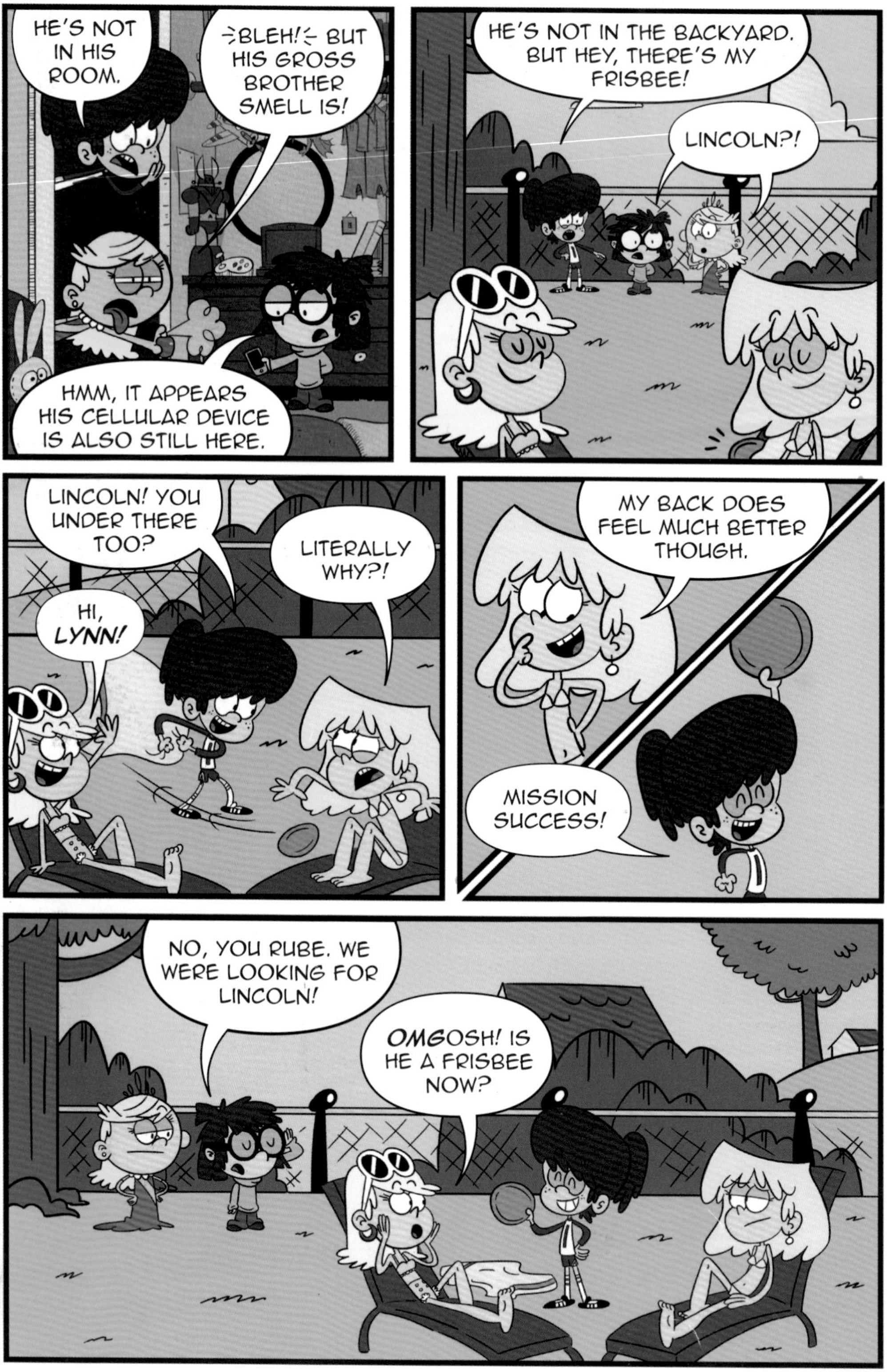
HE'S NOT IN HIS ROOM.
BLEH! BUT HIS GROSS BROTHER SMELL IS!
HMM, IT APPEARS HIS CELLULAR DEVICE IS ALSO STILL HERE.
HE'S NOT IN THE BACKYARD. BUT HEY, THERE'S MY FRISBEE!
LINCOLN?!
LINCOLN! YOU UNDER THERE TOO?
LITERALLY WHY?!
HI, *LYNN!*
MY BACK DOES FEEL MUCH BETTER THOUGH.
MISSION SUCCESS!
NO, YOU RUBE. WE WERE LOOKING FOR LINCOLN!
*OMG*OSH! IS HE A FRISBEE NOW?

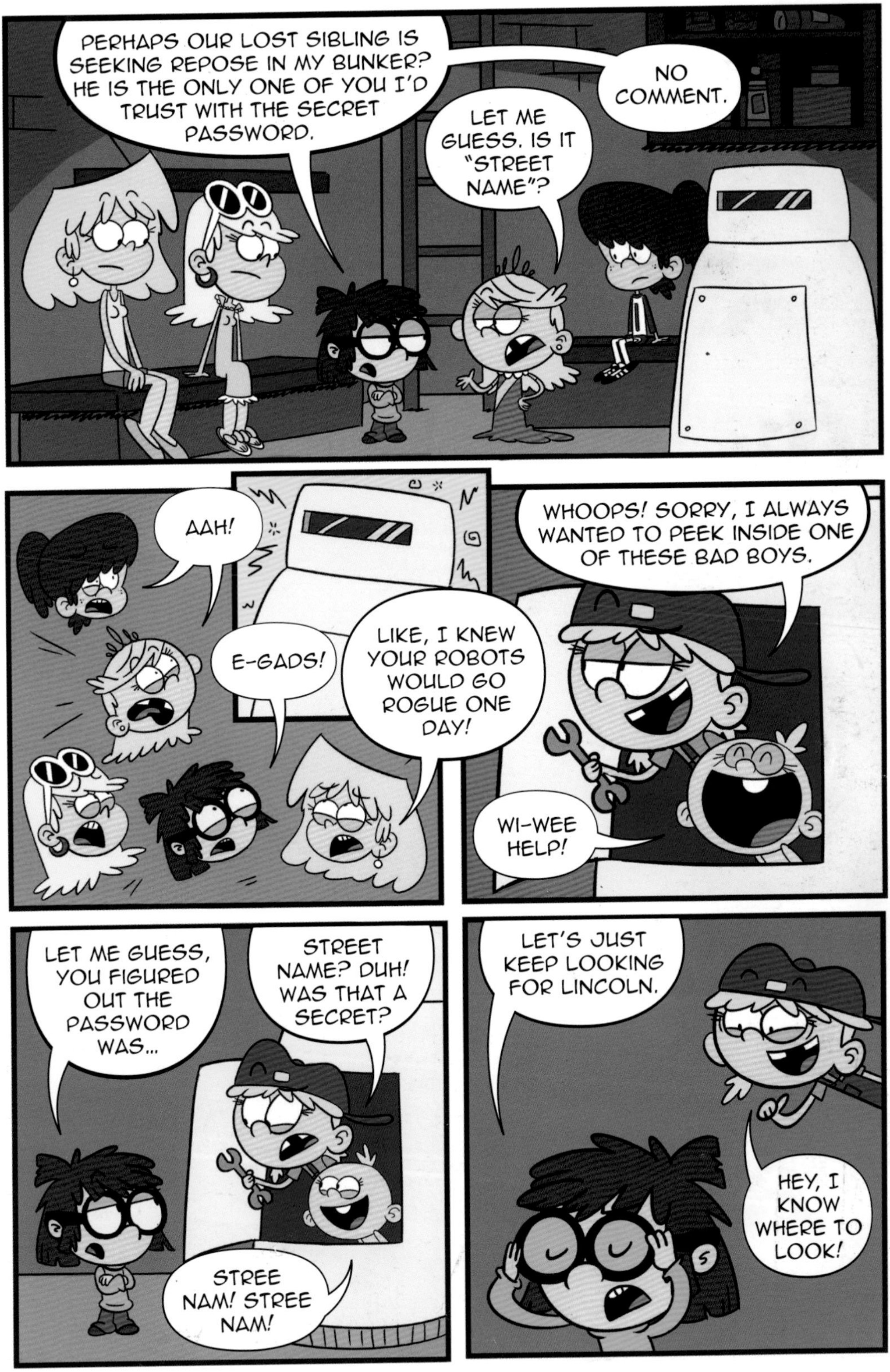
PERHAPS OUR LOST SIBLING IS SEEKING REPOSE IN MY BUNKER? HE IS THE ONLY ONE OF YOU I'D TRUST WITH THE SECRET PASSWORD.
NO COMMENT.
LET ME GUESS. IS IT "STREET NAME"?
AAH!
E-GADS!
LIKE, I KNEW YOUR ROBOTS WOULD GO ROGUE ONE DAY!
WHOOPS! SORRY, I ALWAYS WANTED TO PEEK INSIDE ONE OF THESE BAD BOYS.
WI-WEE HELP!
LET ME GUESS, YOU FIGURED OUT THE PASSWORD WAS...
STREET NAME? DUH! WAS THAT A SECRET?
STREE NAM! STREE NAM!
LET'S JUST KEEP LOOKING FOR LINCOLN.
HEY, I KNOW WHERE TO LOOK!

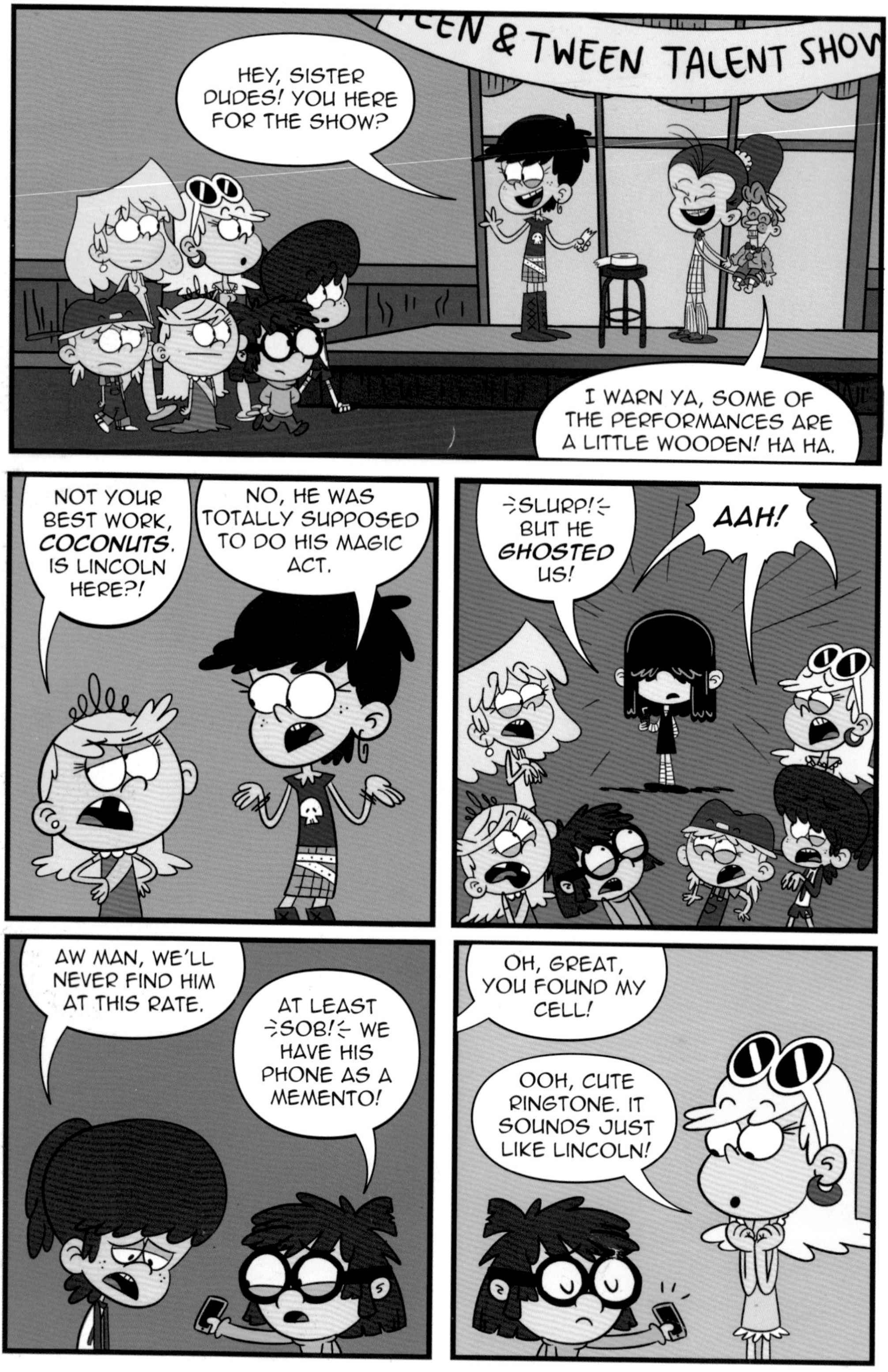
TEEN & TWEEN TALENT SHOW
HEY, SISTER DUDES! YOU HERE FOR THE SHOW?
I WARN YA, SOME OF THE PERFORMANCES ARE A LITTLE WOODEN! HA HA.
NOT YOUR BEST WORK, COCONUTS. IS LINCOLN HERE?!
NO, HE WAS TOTALLY SUPPOSED TO DO HIS MAGIC ACT.
SLURP! BUT HE GHOSTED US!
AAH!
AW MAN, WE'LL NEVER FIND HIM AT THIS RATE.
AT LEAST SOB! WE HAVE HIS PHONE AS A MEMENTO!
OH, GREAT, YOU FOUND MY CELL!
OOH, CUTE RINGTONE. IT SOUNDS JUST LIKE LINCOLN!

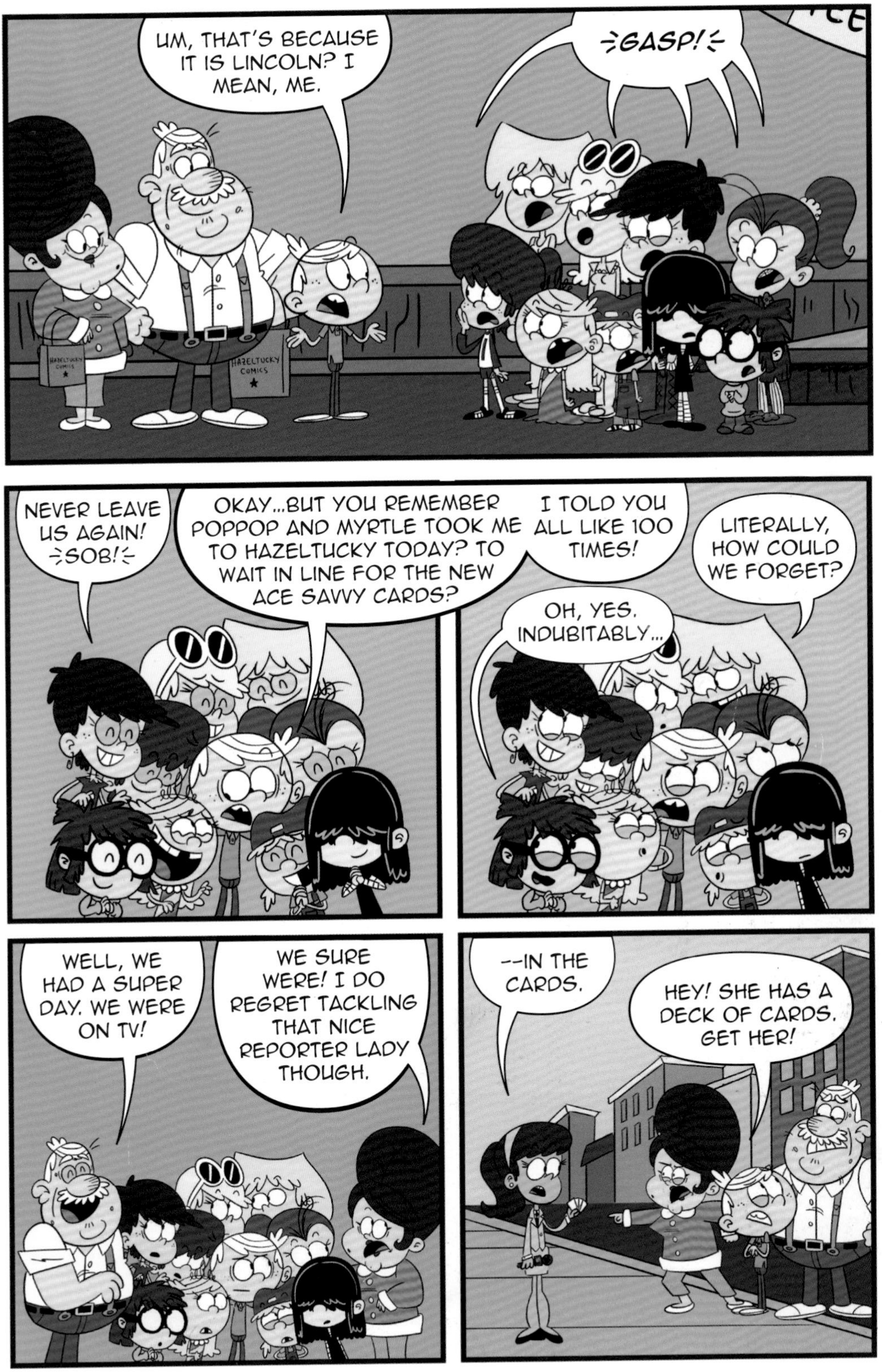
UM, THAT'S BECAUSE IT IS LINCOLN? I MEAN, ME.
GASP!
HAZELTUCKY COMICS
NEVER LEAVE US AGAIN! SOB!
OKAY...BUT YOU REMEMBER POPPOP AND MYRTLE TOOK ME TO HAZELTUCKY TODAY? TO WAIT IN LINE FOR THE NEW ACE SAVVY CARDS?
I TOLD YOU ALL LIKE 100 TIMES!
LITERALLY, HOW COULD WE FORGET?
OH, YES. INDUBITABLY...
WELL, WE HAD A SUPER DAY. WE WERE ON TV!
WE SURE WERE! I DO REGRET TACKLING THAT NICE REPORTER LADY THOUGH.
--IN THE CARDS.
HEY! SHE HAS A DECK OF CARDS. GET HER!

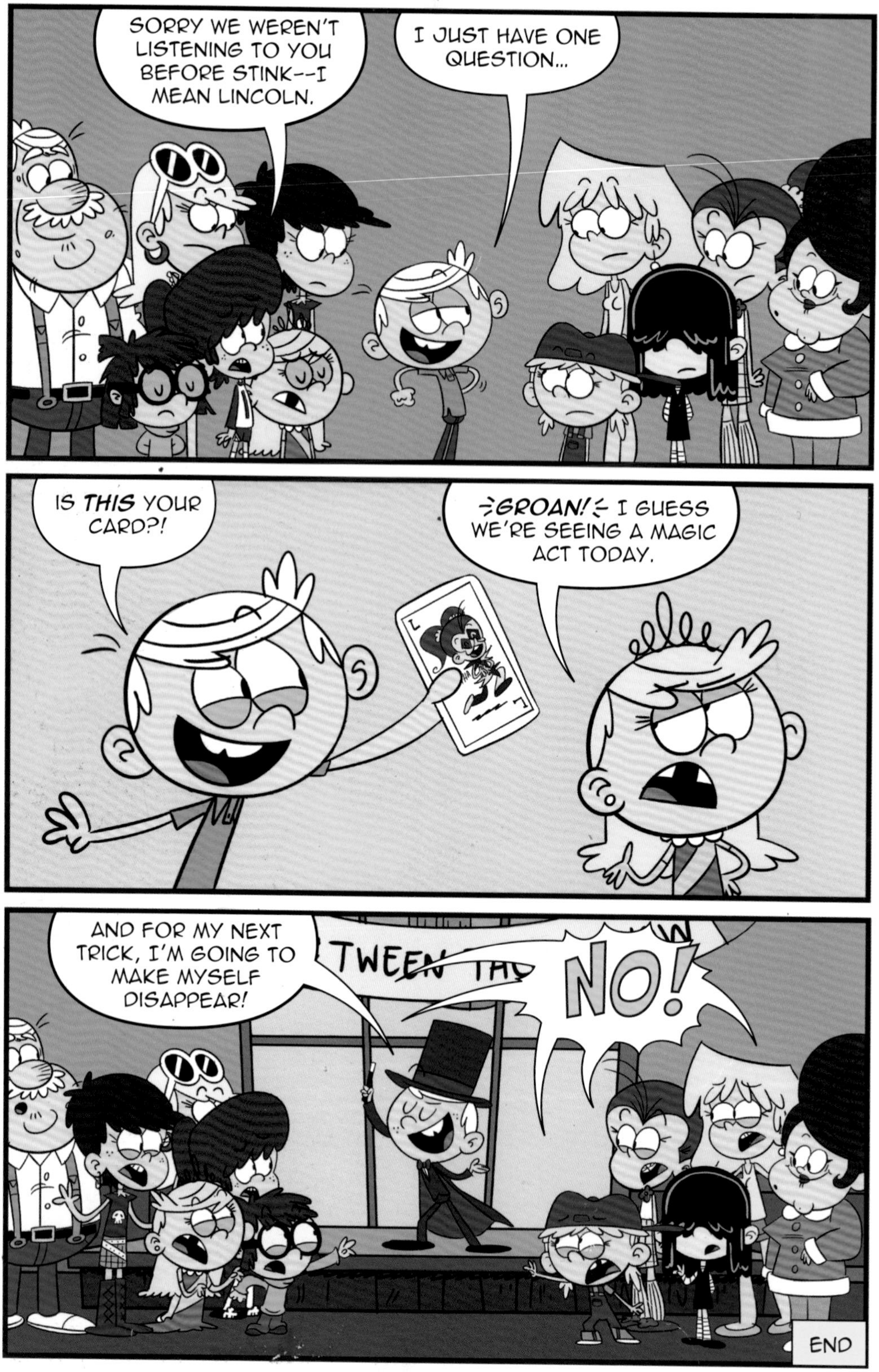

SORRY WE WEREN'T LISTENING TO YOU BEFORE STINK--I MEAN LINCOLN.
I JUST HAVE ONE QUESTION...
IS *THIS* YOUR CARD?!
GROAN! I GUESS WE'RE SEEING A MAGIC ACT TODAY.
AND FOR MY NEXT TRICK, I'M GOING TO MAKE MYSELF DISAPPEAR!
TWEEN
NO!
END

"I BELIEVE"

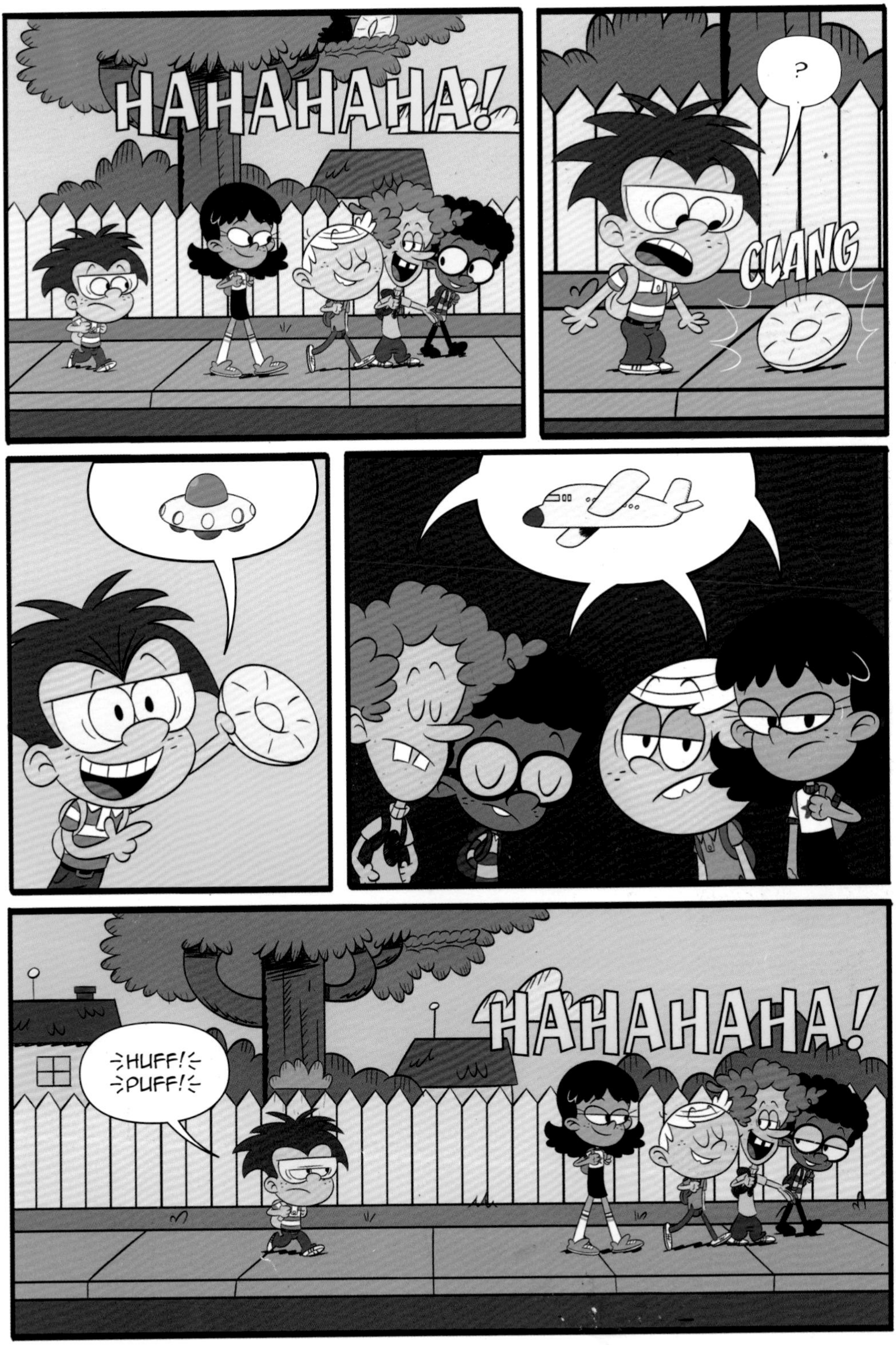
HAHAHAHA!
?
CLANG
HAHAHAHA!
HUFF! PUFF!

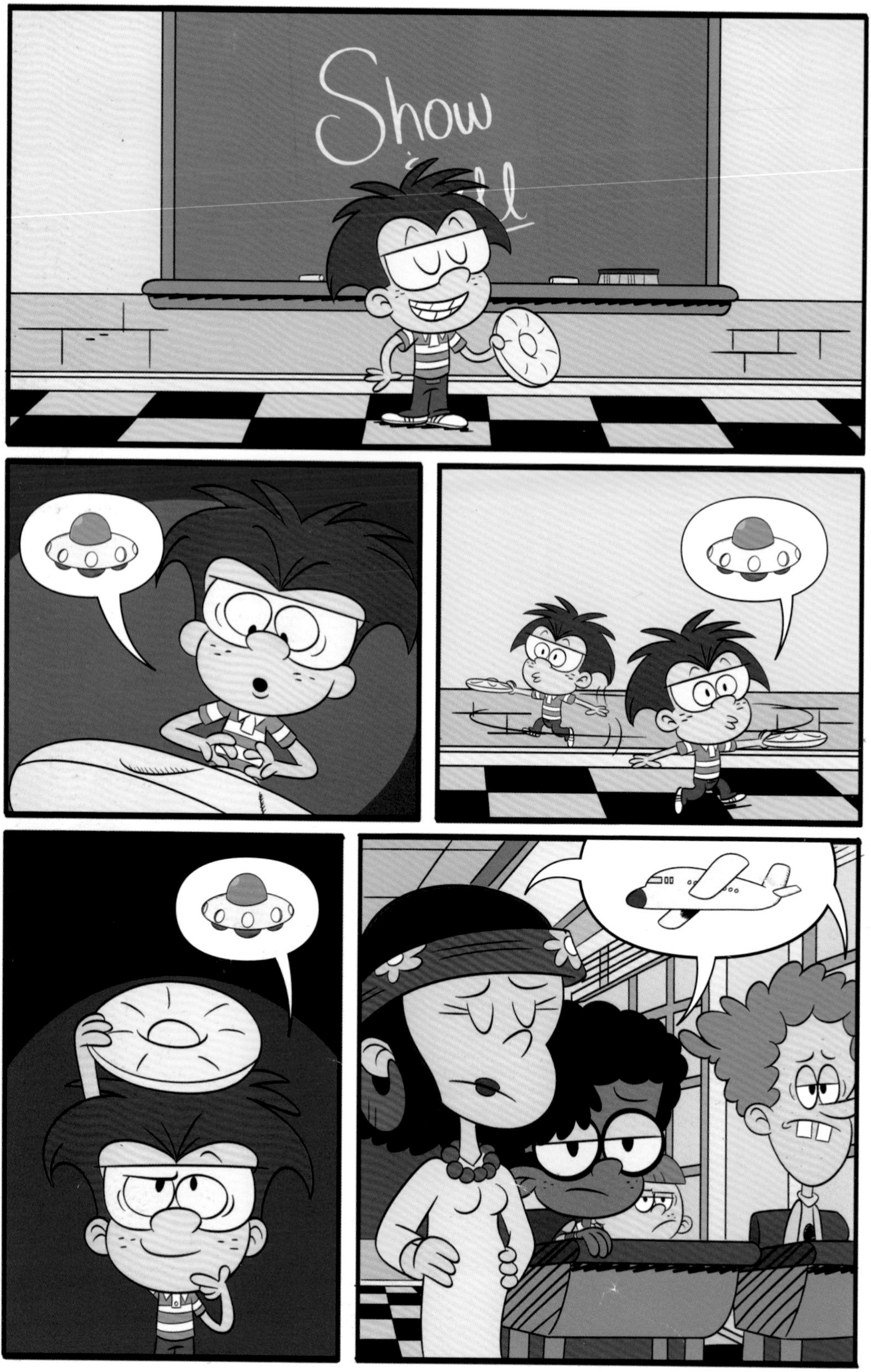
Show

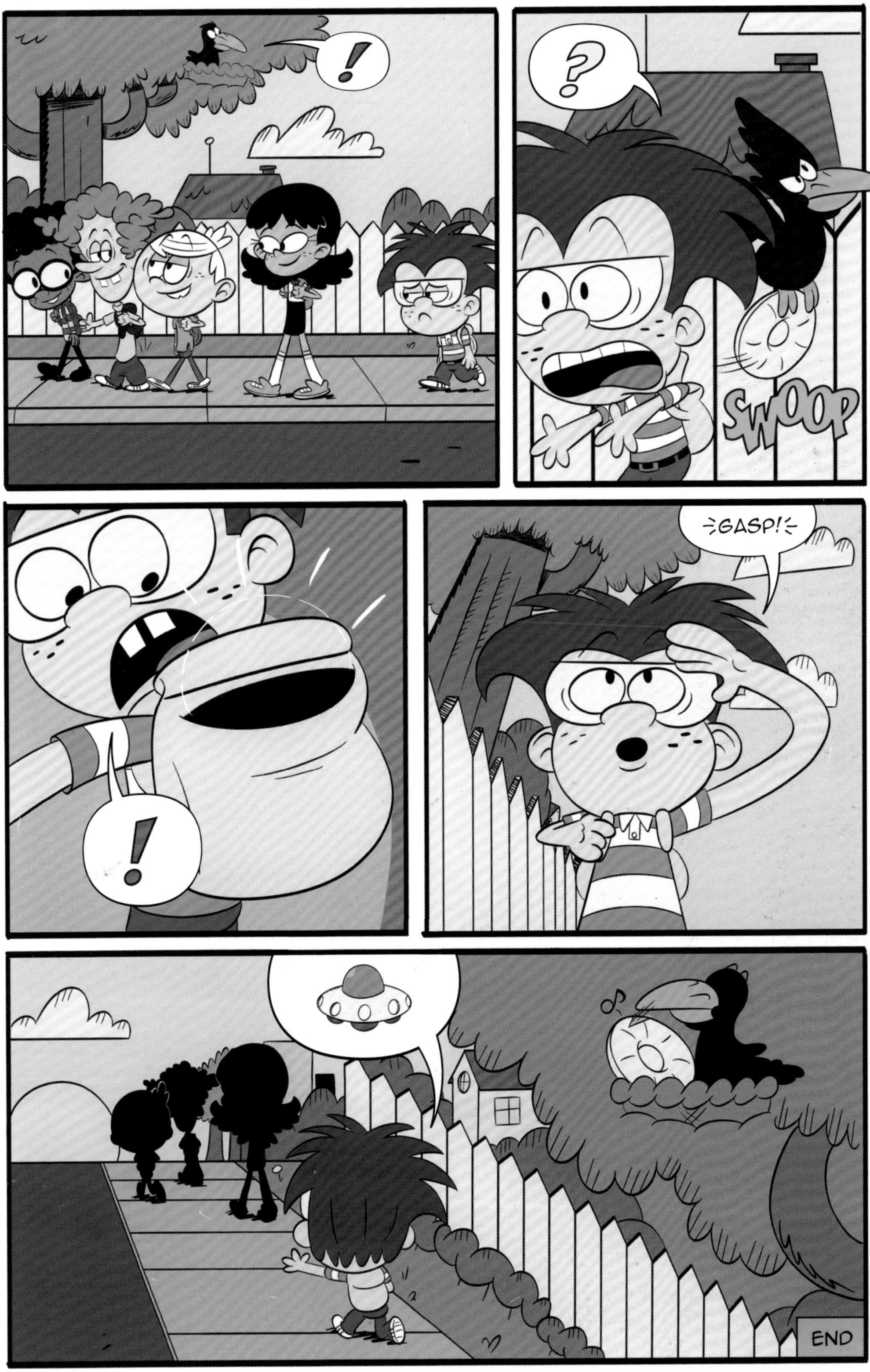
!
?
SWOOP
!
GASP!
END

"AN UNDEAD DEBATE"

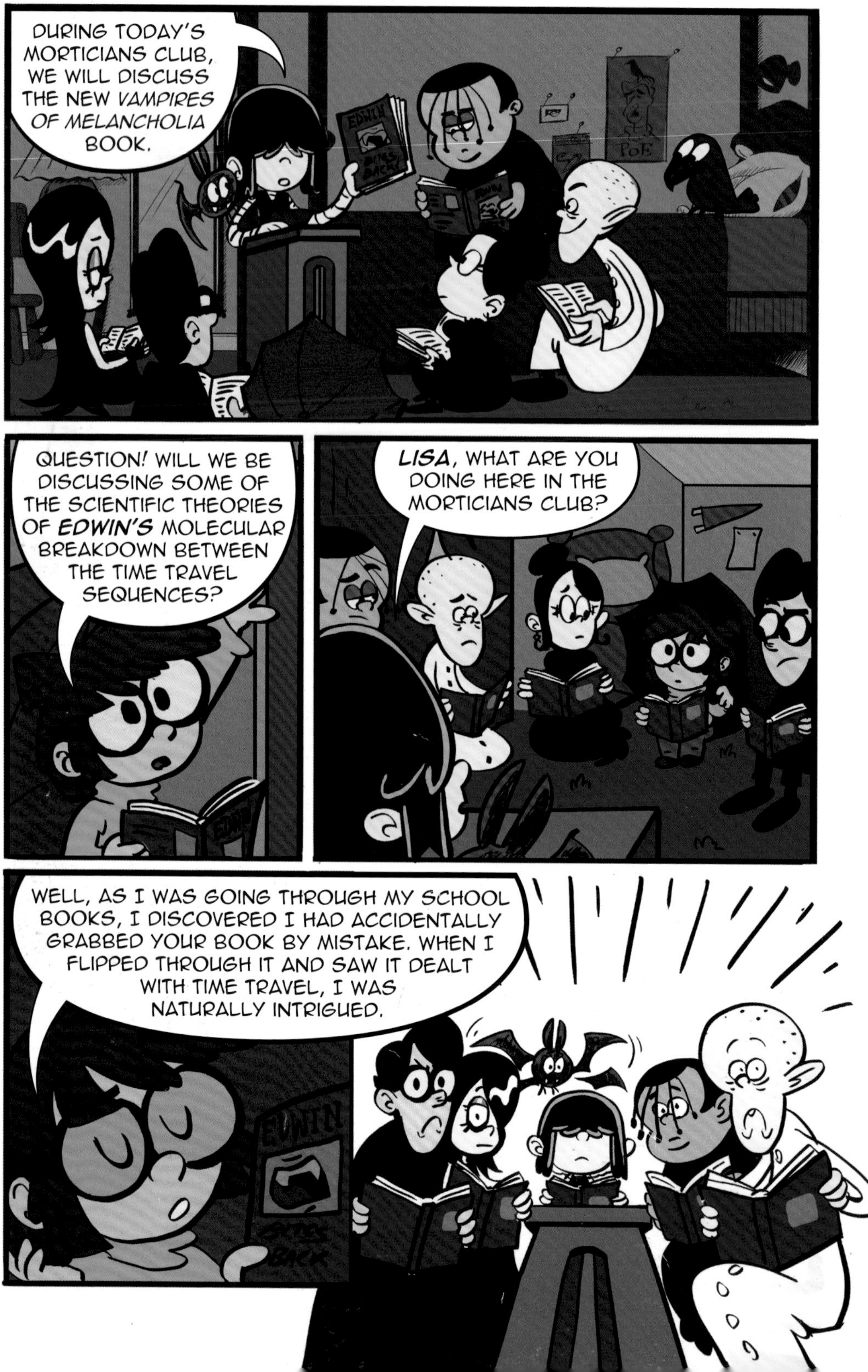

DURING TODAY'S MORTICIANS CLUB, WE WILL DISCUSS THE NEW VAMPIRES OF MELANCHOLIA BOOK.
EDWIN BITES BACK!
POE
QUESTION! WILL WE BE DISCUSSING SOME OF THE SCIENTIFIC THEORIES OF EDWIN'S MOLECULAR BREAKDOWN BETWEEN THE TIME TRAVEL SEQUENCES?
LISA, WHAT ARE YOU DOING HERE IN THE MORTICIANS CLUB?
WELL, AS I WAS GOING THROUGH MY SCHOOL BOOKS, I DISCOVERED I HAD ACCIDENTALLY GRABBED YOUR BOOK BY MISTAKE. WHEN I FLIPPED THROUGH IT AND SAW IT DEALT WITH TIME TRAVEL, I WAS NATURALLY INTRIGUED.
EDWIN BITES BACK

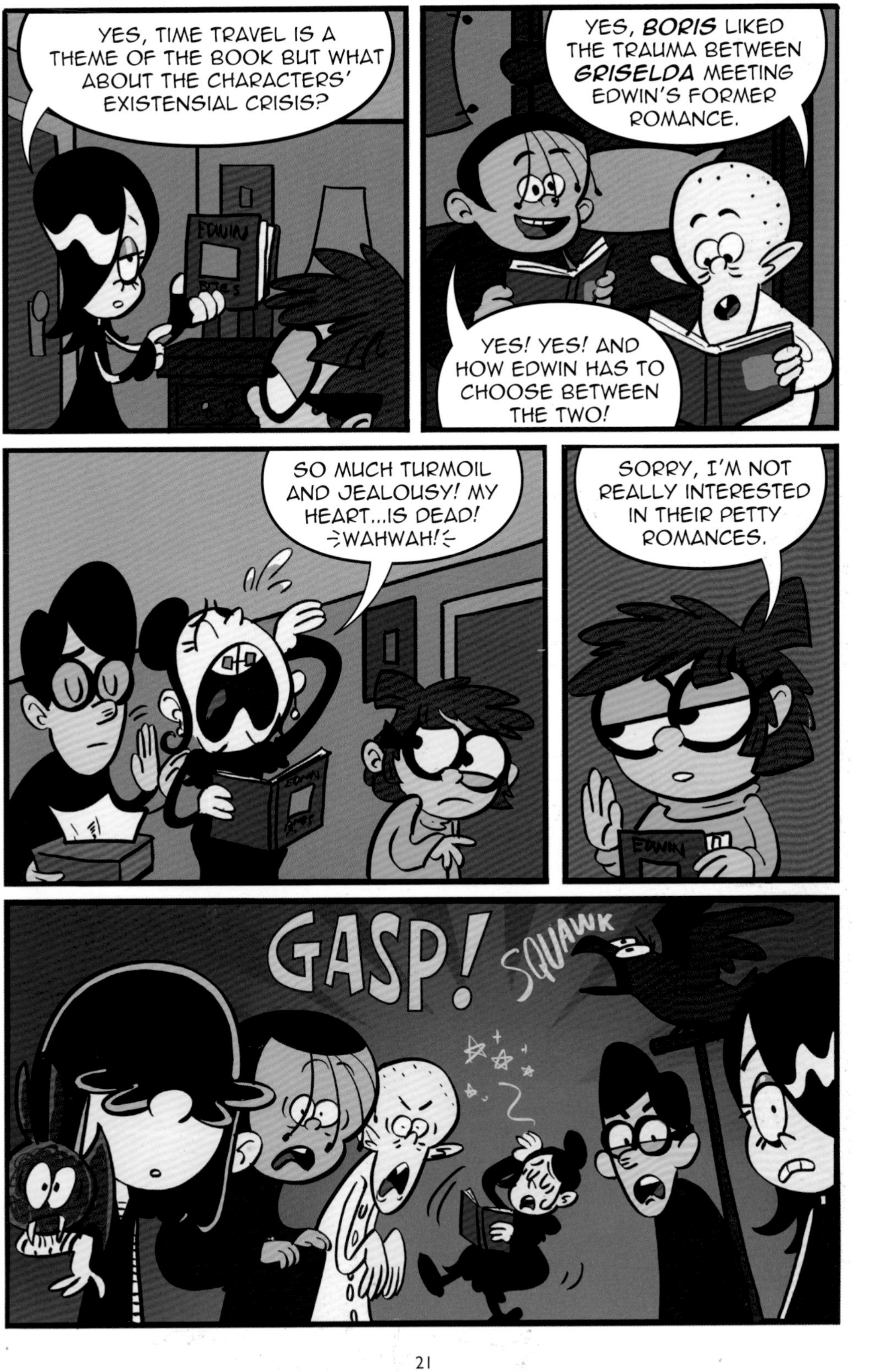
YES, TIME TRAVEL IS A THEME OF THE BOOK BUT WHAT ABOUT THE CHARACTERS' EXISTENSIAL CRISIS?
EDWIN
YES, BORIS LIKED THE TRAUMA BETWEEN GRISELDA MEETING EDWIN'S FORMER ROMANCE.
YES! YES! AND HOW EDWIN HAS TO CHOOSE BETWEEN THE TWO!
SO MUCH TURMOIL AND JEALOUSY! MY HEART...IS DEAD! WAHWAH!
EDWIN
SORRY, I'M NOT REALLY INTERESTED IN THEIR PETTY ROMANCES.
EDWIN
GASP!
SQUAWK

DON'T LISTEN TO HER, EDWIN!

DID I SAY SOMETHING WRONG?

LISA, THE VERY GOTHIC AND CONTROVERSIAL ROMANCE OF THE NOVEL...

BANG BANG

...*IS* AN IMPORTANT CLUB DISCUSSION. IT'S WHAT WE *DIE* FOR.

I DON'T QUITE UNDERSTAND WHAT THERE IS TO DISCUSS. ACCORDING TO MY CALCULATIONS... HIT THE LIGHTS, IF YOU WILL?

SCREECH SCREECH

IT'S LOGICALLY ACCURATE TO SAY EDWIN AND HIS FORMER LOVE *MISS BELLATRIX* ARE MORE COMPATIBLE TOGETHER.

GRISELDA = MELANCHOLY?

MISS BELLATRIX + DARKNESS = LIGHT

LIGHT / DARK = GREY

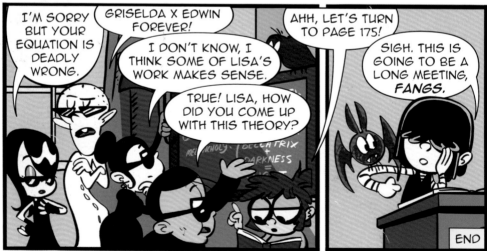

I'M SORRY BUT YOUR EQUATION IS DEADLY WRONG.

GRISELDA X EDWIN FOREVER!

I DON'T KNOW, I THINK SOME OF LISA'S WORK MAKES SENSE.

TRUE! LISA, HOW DID YOU COME UP WITH THIS THEORY?

AHH, LET'S TURN TO PAGE 175!

SIGH. THIS IS GOING TO BE A LONG MEETING, *FANGS.*

END

"MALL TRIP"

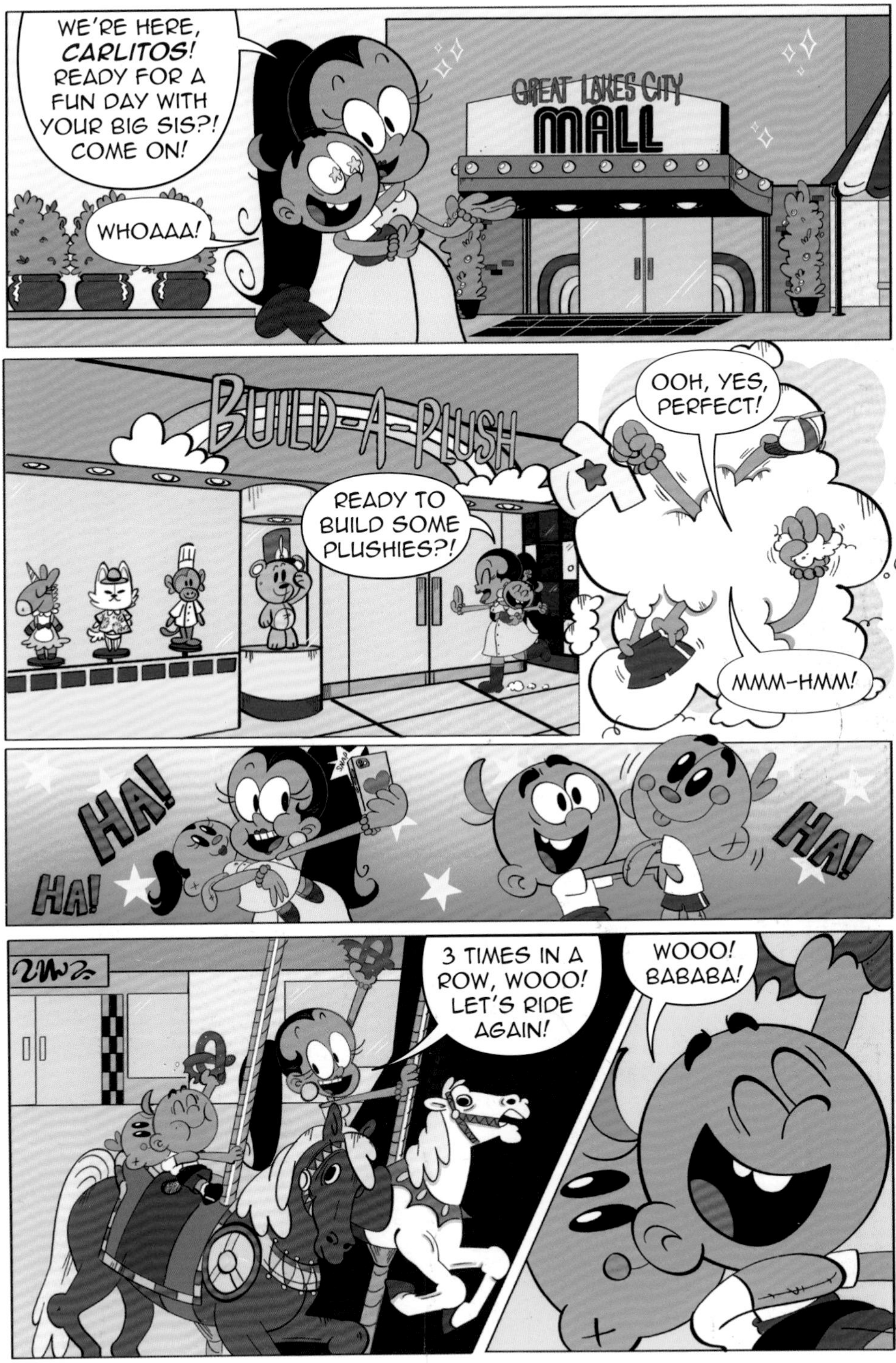
WE'RE HERE, CARLITOS! READY FOR A FUN DAY WITH YOUR BIG SIS?! COME ON!
GREAT LAKES CITY MALL
WHOAAA!
BUILD-A-PLUSH
READY TO BUILD SOME PLUSHIES?!
OOH, YES, PERFECT!
MMM-HMM!
HA!
HA!
HA!
3 TIMES IN A ROW, WOOO! LET'S RIDE AGAIN!
WOOO! BABABA!

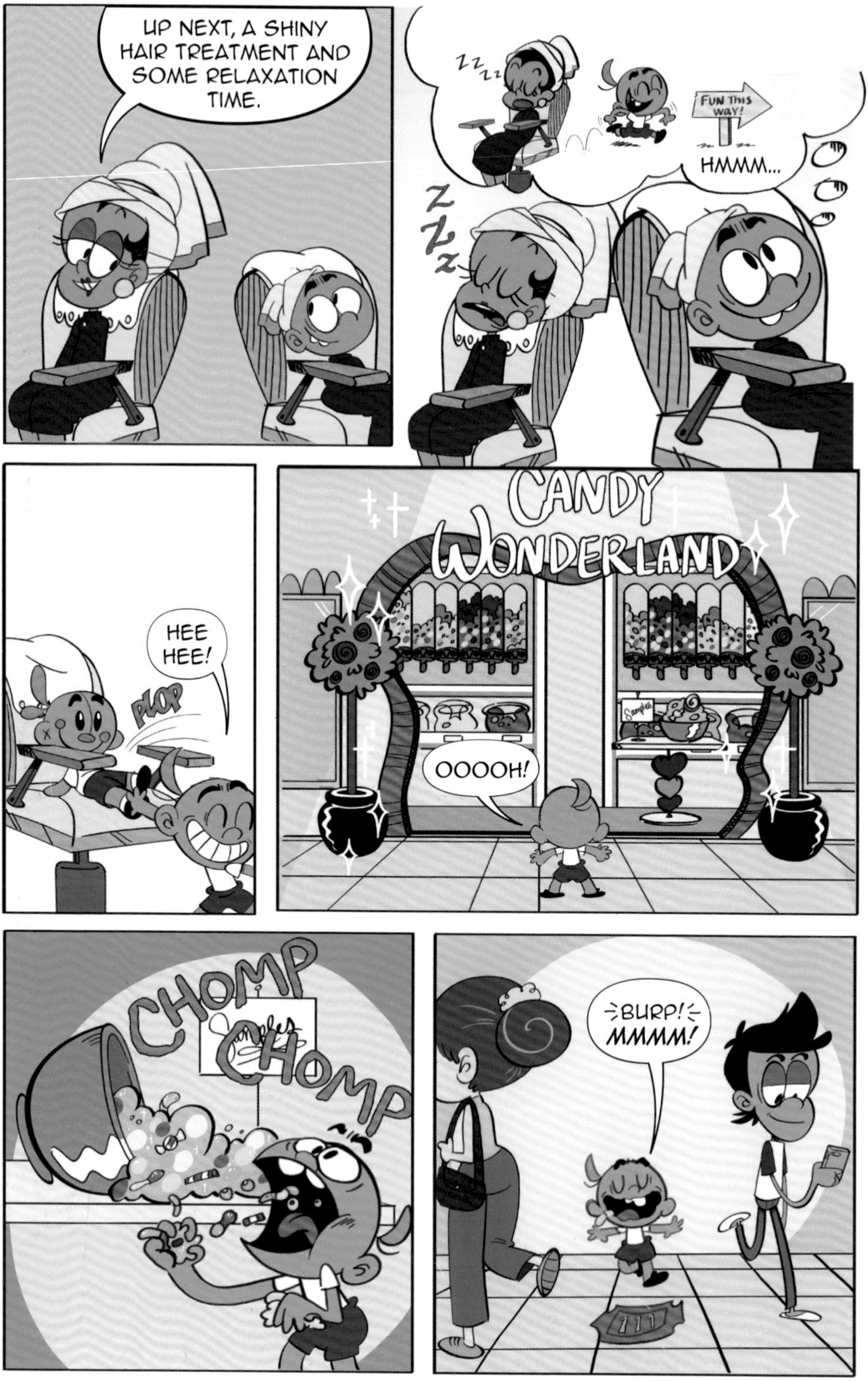
UP NEXT, A SHINY HAIR TREATMENT AND SOME RELAXATION TIME.
FUN THIS WAY!
HMMM...
HEE HEE!
PLOP
CANDY WONDERLAND
Samples
OOOOH!
CHOMP
CHOMP
BURP!
MMMM!

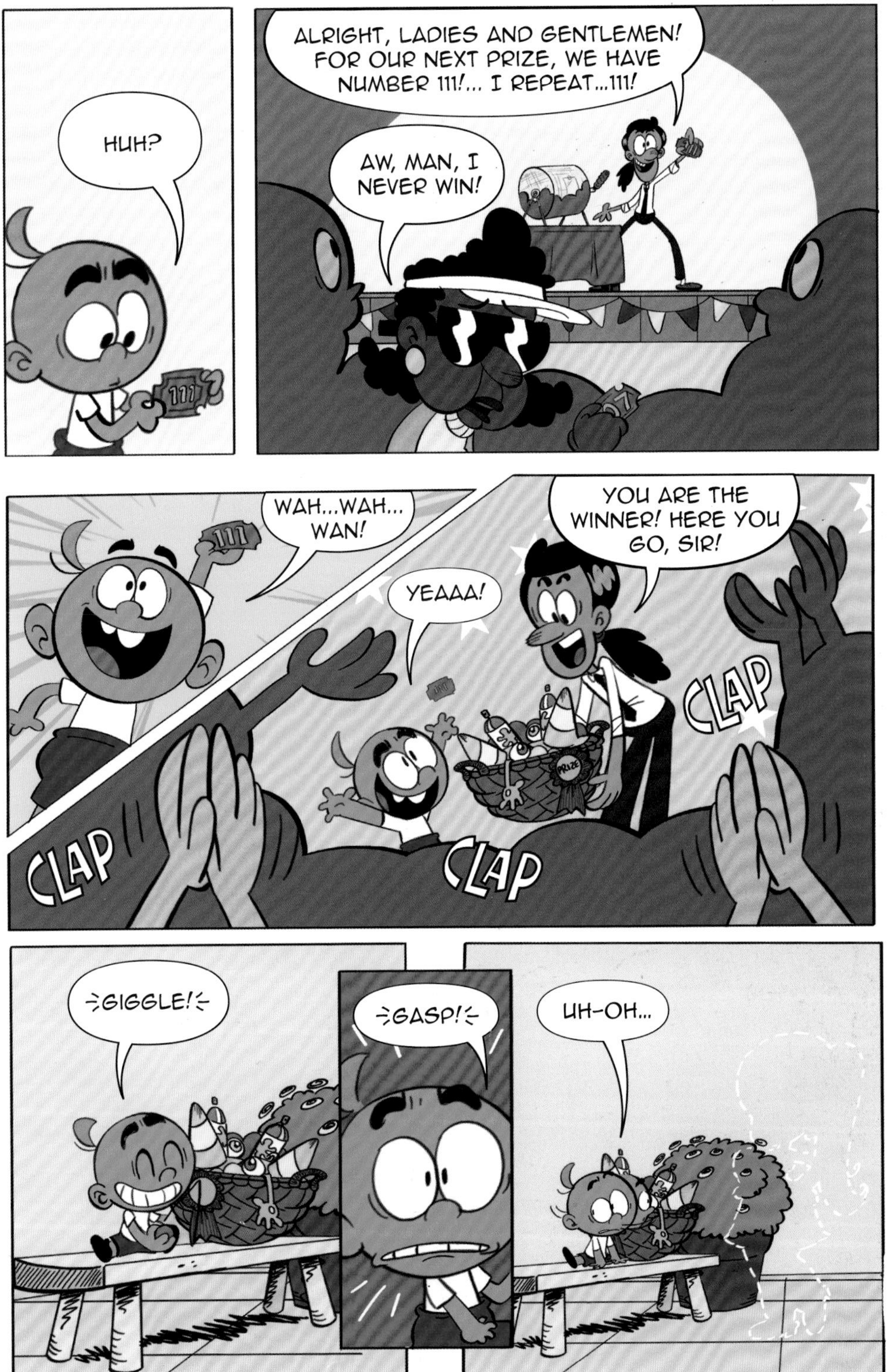
HUH?
ALRIGHT, LADIES AND GENTLEMEN! FOR OUR NEXT PRIZE, WE HAVE NUMBER 111!... I REPEAT...111!
AW, MAN, I NEVER WIN!
WAH...WAH... WAN!
YOU ARE THE WINNER! HERE YOU GO, SIR!
YEAAA!
CLAP
CLAP
CLAP
GIGGLE!
GASP!
UH-OH...

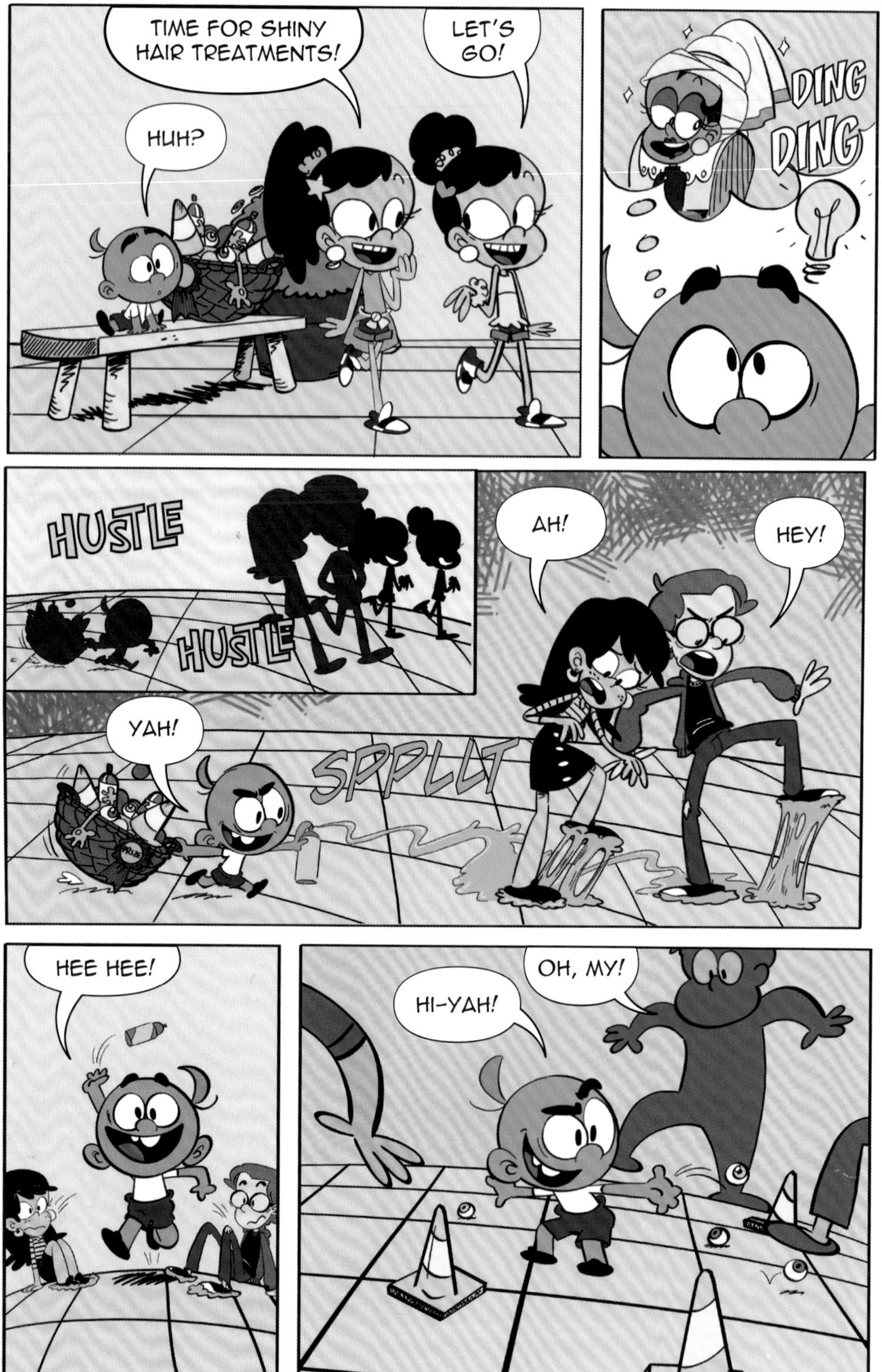
HUH?
TIME FOR SHINY HAIR TREATMENTS!
LET'S GO!
DING
DING
HUSTLE
HUSTLE
AH!
HEY!
YAH!
SPPLLT
HEE HEE!
HI-YAH!
OH, MY!

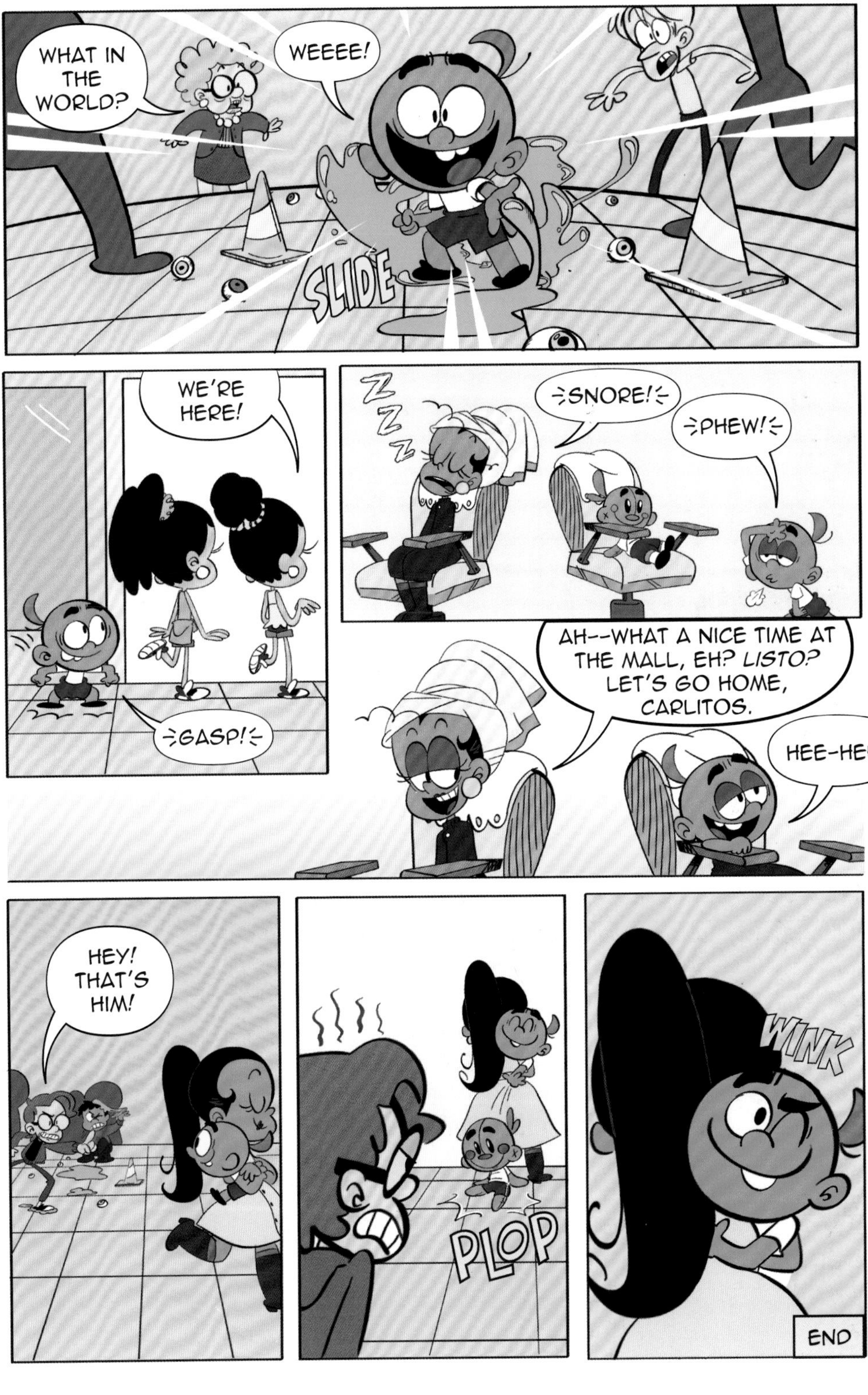
WHAT IN THE WORLD?
WEEEE!
SLIDE
WE'RE HERE!
GASP!
SNORE!
PHEW!
AH--WHAT A NICE TIME AT THE MALL, EH? *LISTO?* LET'S GO HOME, CARLITOS.
HEE-HEE!
HEY! THAT'S HIM!
PLOP
WINK
END

"PLAYING TO THE CROWD"

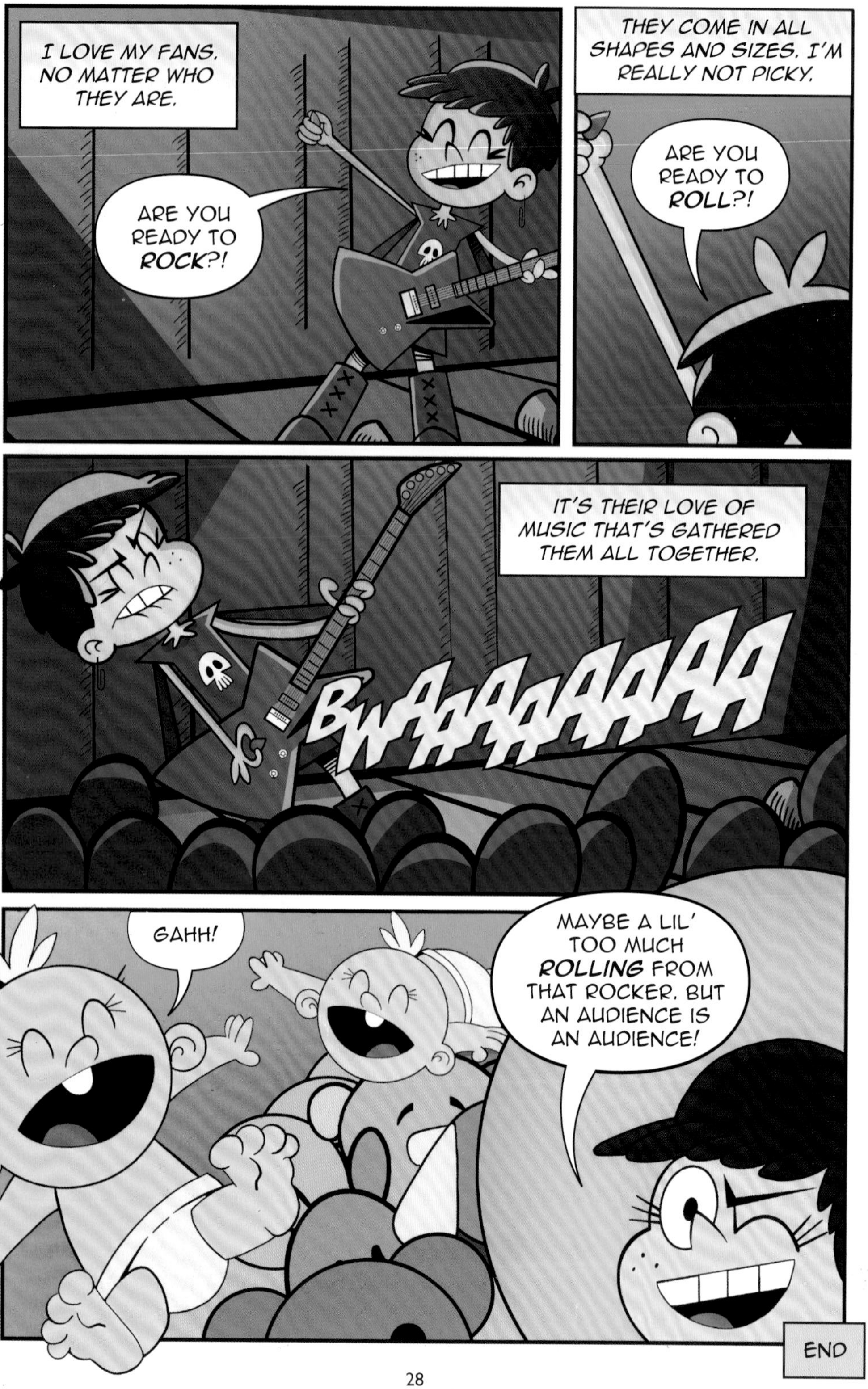
I LOVE MY FANS, NO MATTER WHO THEY ARE.
ARE YOU READY TO ROCK?!
THEY COME IN ALL SHAPES AND SIZES. I'M REALLY NOT PICKY.
ARE YOU READY TO ROLL?!
IT'S THEIR LOVE OF MUSIC THAT'S GATHERED THEM ALL TOGETHER.
BWAAAAAAAAA
GAHH!
MAYBE A LIL' TOO MUCH ROLLING FROM THAT ROCKER, BUT AN AUDIENCE IS AN AUDIENCE!
END

"CONSTRUCTION CONUNDRUM"

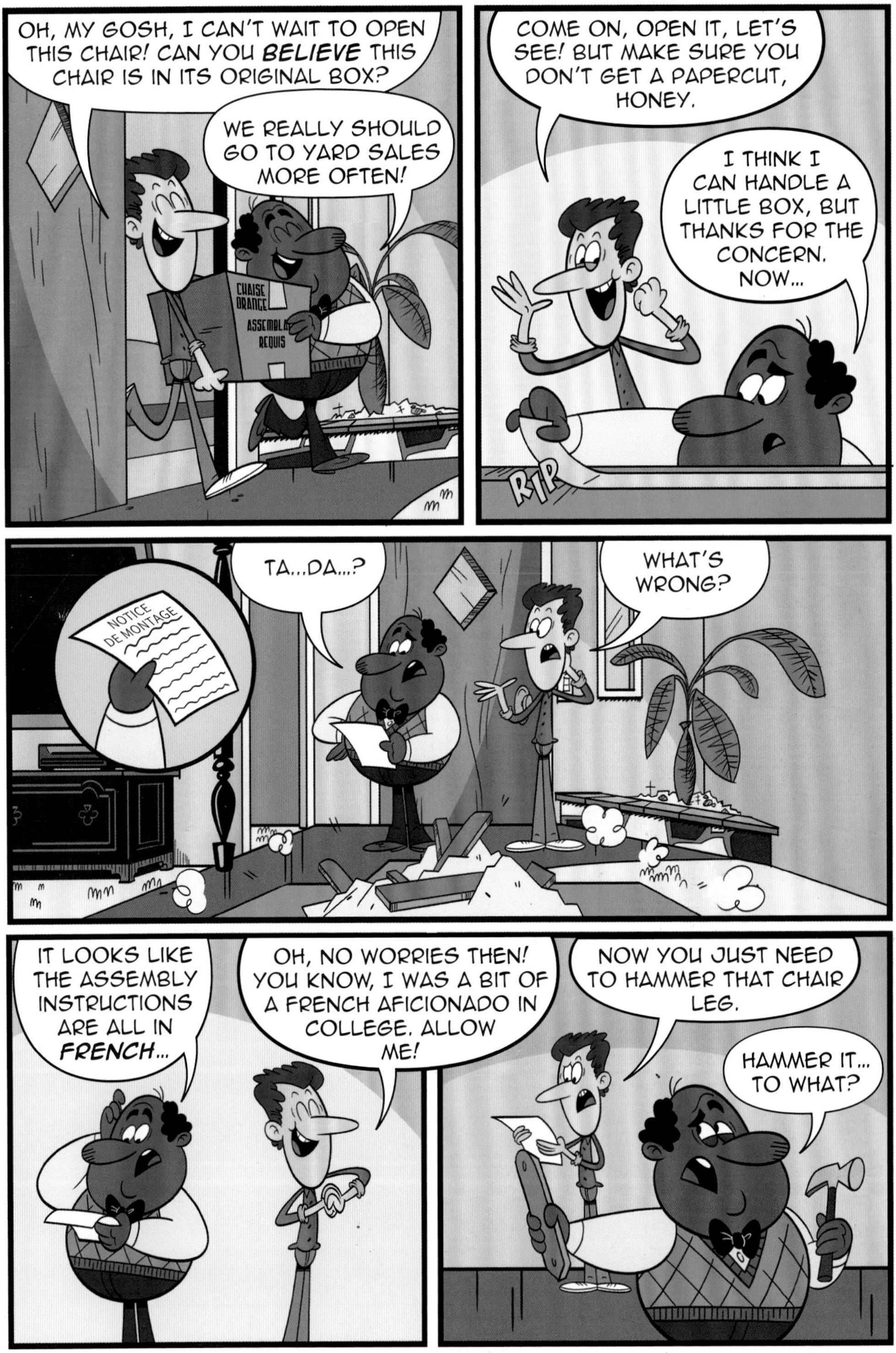

OH, MY GOSH, I CAN'T WAIT TO OPEN THIS CHAIR! CAN YOU *BELIEVE* THIS CHAIR IS IN ITS ORIGINAL BOX?
WE REALLY SHOULD GO TO YARD SALES MORE OFTEN!
CHAISE ORANGE
ASSEMBL REQUIS
COME ON, OPEN IT, LET'S SEE! BUT MAKE SURE YOU DON'T GET A PAPERCUT, HONEY.
I THINK I CAN HANDLE A LITTLE BOX, BUT THANKS FOR THE CONCERN. NOW...
RIP
NOTICE DE MONTAGE
TA...DA...?
WHAT'S WRONG?
IT LOOKS LIKE THE ASSEMBLY INSTRUCTIONS ARE ALL IN *FRENCH*...
OH, NO WORRIES THEN! YOU KNOW, I WAS A BIT OF A FRENCH AFICIONADO IN COLLEGE. ALLOW ME!
NOW YOU JUST NEED TO HAMMER THAT CHAIR LEG.
HAMMER IT... TO WHAT?

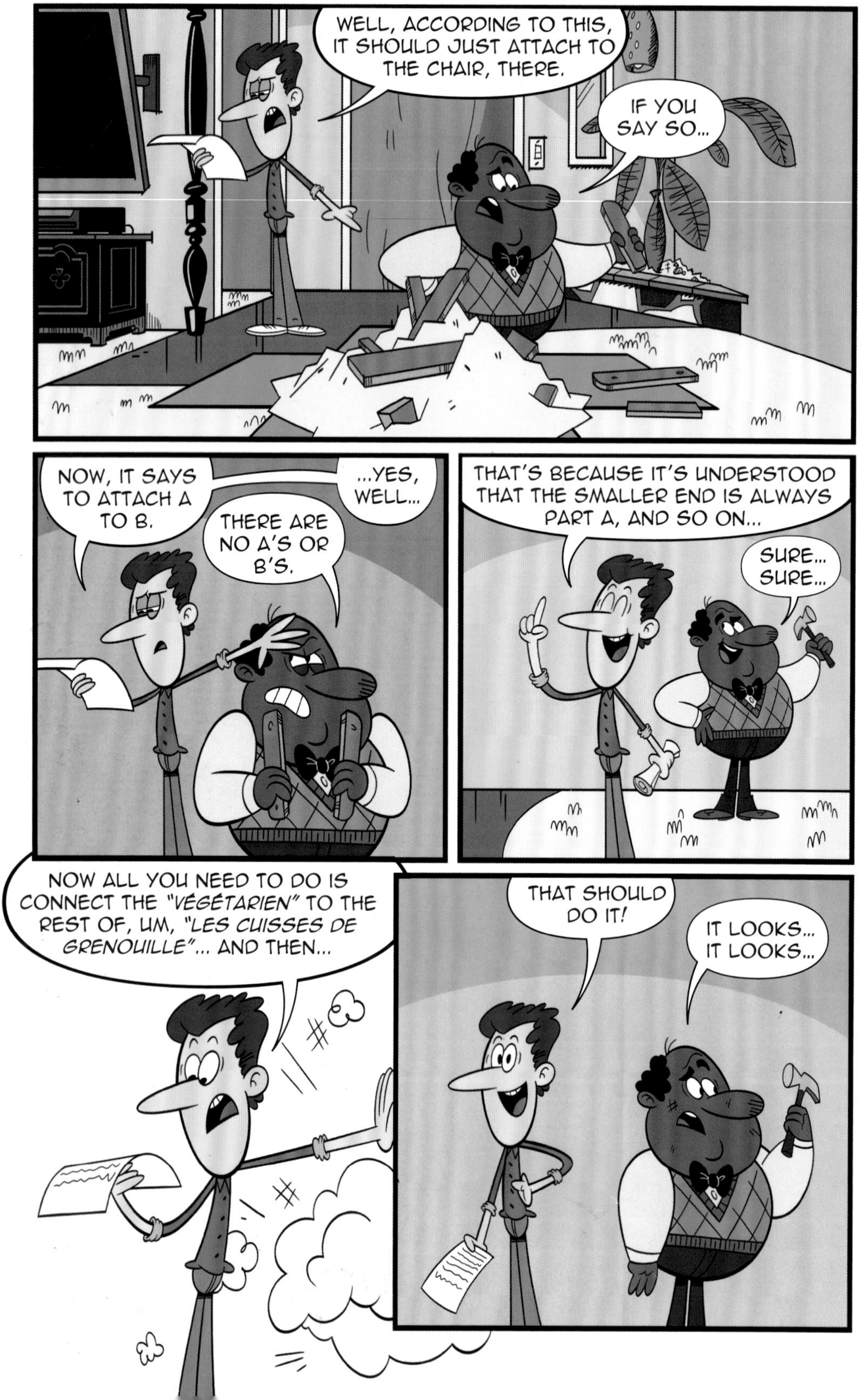
WELL, ACCORDING TO THIS, IT SHOULD JUST ATTACH TO THE CHAIR, THERE.
IF YOU SAY SO...
NOW, IT SAYS TO ATTACH A TO B.
THERE ARE NO A'S OR B'S.
...YES, WELL...
THAT'S BECAUSE IT'S UNDERSTOOD THAT THE SMALLER END IS ALWAYS PART A, AND SO ON...
SURE... SURE...
NOW ALL YOU NEED TO DO IS CONNECT THE "*VÉGÉTARIEN*" TO THE REST OF, UM, "*LES CUISSES DE GRENOUILLE*"... AND THEN...
THAT SHOULD DO IT!
IT LOOKS... IT LOOKS...

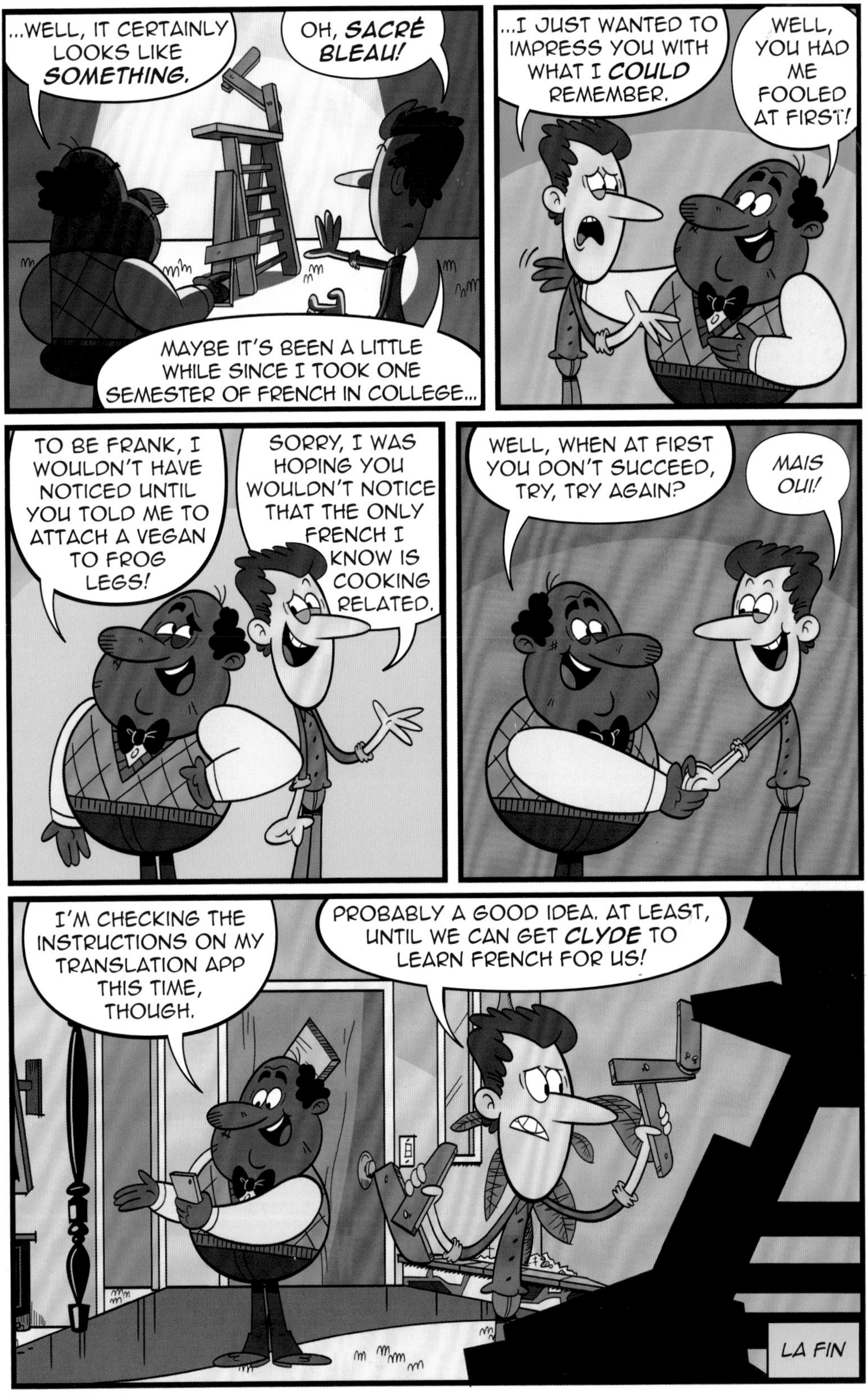
...WELL, IT CERTAINLY LOOKS LIKE *SOMETHING.*
OH, *SACRÉ BLEAU!*
MAYBE IT'S BEEN A LITTLE WHILE SINCE I TOOK ONE SEMESTER OF FRENCH IN COLLEGE...
...I JUST WANTED TO IMPRESS YOU WITH WHAT I *COULD* REMEMBER.
WELL, YOU HAD ME FOOLED AT FIRST!
TO BE FRANK, I WOULDN'T HAVE NOTICED UNTIL YOU TOLD ME TO ATTACH A VEGAN TO FROG LEGS!
SORRY, I WAS HOPING YOU WOULDN'T NOTICE THAT THE ONLY FRENCH I KNOW IS COOKING RELATED.
WELL, WHEN AT FIRST YOU DON'T SUCCEED, TRY, TRY AGAIN?
MAIS OUI!
I'M CHECKING THE INSTRUCTIONS ON MY TRANSLATION APP THIS TIME, THOUGH.
PROBABLY A GOOD IDEA. AT LEAST, UNTIL WE CAN GET *CLYDE* TO LEARN FRENCH FOR US!
LA FIN

"THE TEAM-UP"

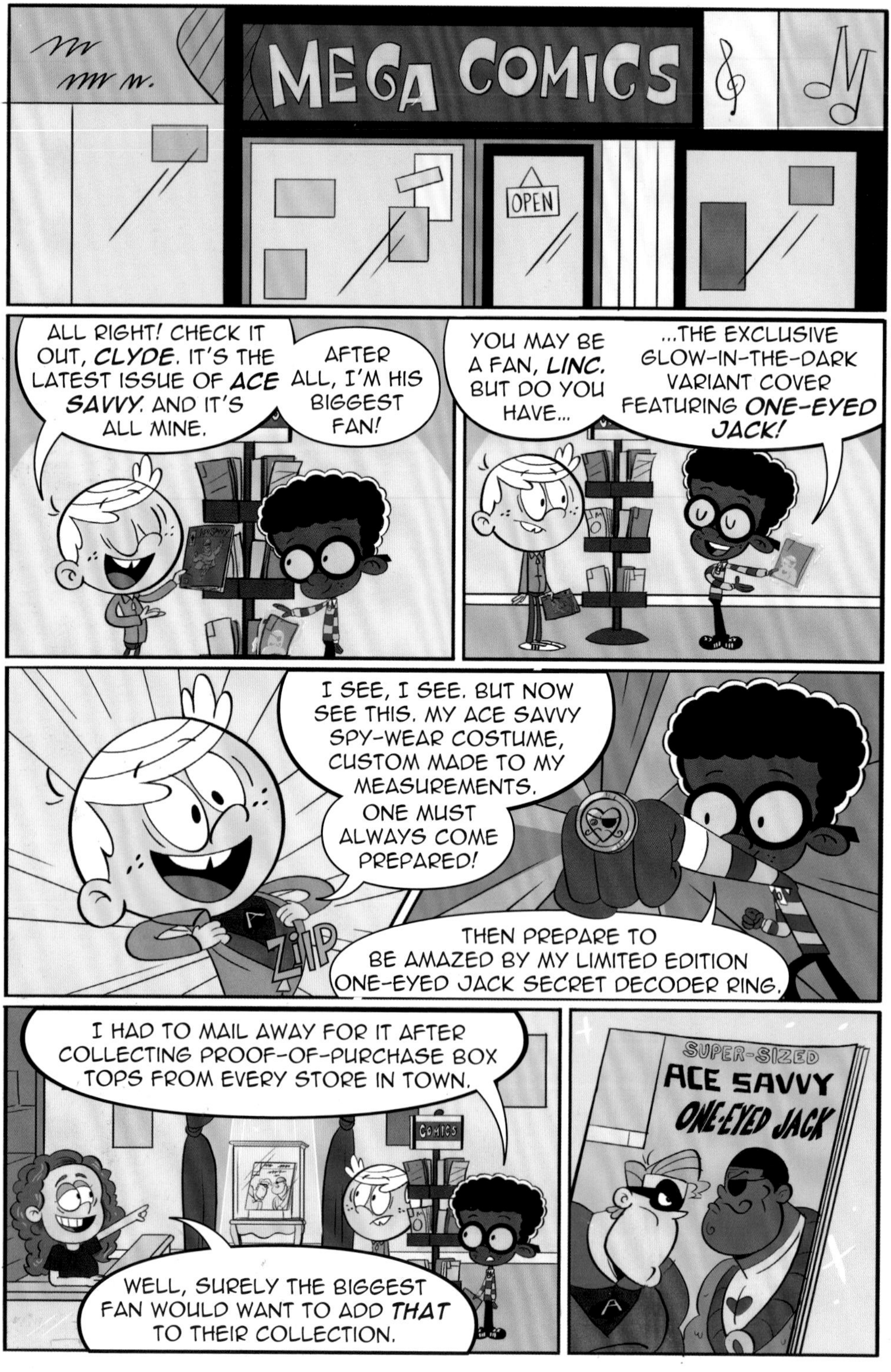
MEGA COMICS
OPEN
ALL RIGHT! CHECK IT OUT, CLYDE. IT'S THE LATEST ISSUE OF ACE SAVVY. AND IT'S ALL MINE.
AFTER ALL, I'M HIS BIGGEST FAN!
YOU MAY BE A FAN, LINC. BUT DO YOU HAVE...
...THE EXCLUSIVE GLOW-IN-THE-DARK VARIANT COVER FEATURING ONE-EYED JACK!
I SEE, I SEE. BUT NOW SEE THIS. MY ACE SAVVY SPY-WEAR COSTUME, CUSTOM MADE TO MY MEASUREMENTS.
ONE MUST ALWAYS COME PREPARED!
ZIIP
THEN PREPARE TO BE AMAZED BY MY LIMITED EDITION ONE-EYED JACK SECRET DECODER RING.
I HAD TO MAIL AWAY FOR IT AFTER COLLECTING PROOF-OF-PURCHASE BOX TOPS FROM EVERY STORE IN TOWN.
COMICS
WELL, SURELY THE BIGGEST FAN WOULD WANT TO ADD THAT TO THEIR COLLECTION.
SUPER-SIZED
ACE SAVVY
ONE-EYED JACK

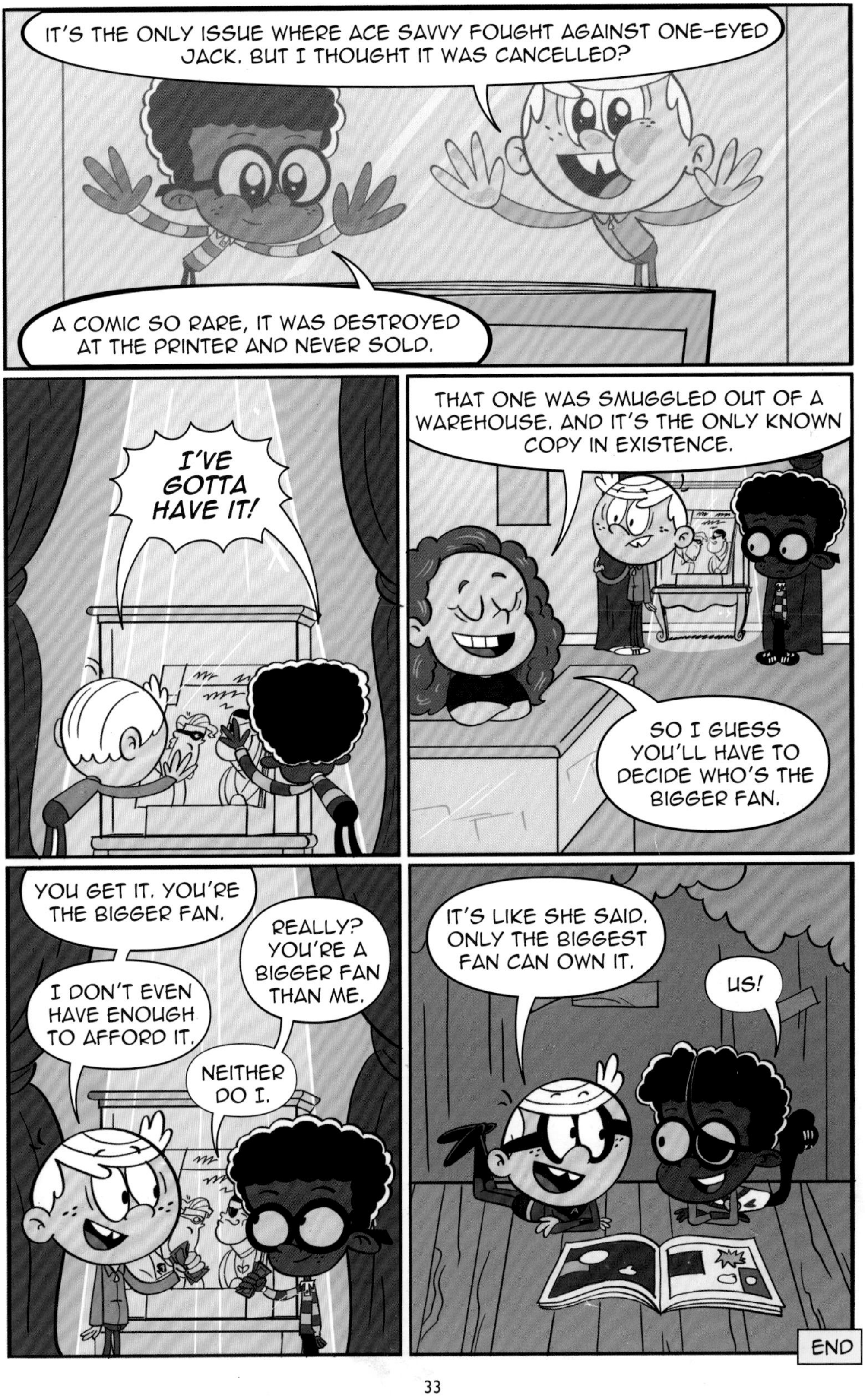
IT'S THE ONLY ISSUE WHERE ACE SAVVY FOUGHT AGAINST ONE-EYED JACK. BUT I THOUGHT IT WAS CANCELLED?
A COMIC SO RARE, IT WAS DESTROYED AT THE PRINTER AND NEVER SOLD.
I'VE GOTTA HAVE IT!
THAT ONE WAS SMUGGLED OUT OF A WAREHOUSE. AND IT'S THE ONLY KNOWN COPY IN EXISTENCE.
SO I GUESS YOU'LL HAVE TO DECIDE WHO'S THE BIGGER FAN.
YOU GET IT. YOU'RE THE BIGGER FAN.
REALLY? YOU'RE A BIGGER FAN THAN ME.
I DON'T EVEN HAVE ENOUGH TO AFFORD IT.
NEITHER DO I.
IT'S LIKE SHE SAID. ONLY THE BIGGEST FAN CAN OWN IT.
US!
END

"SISTER NATURE"

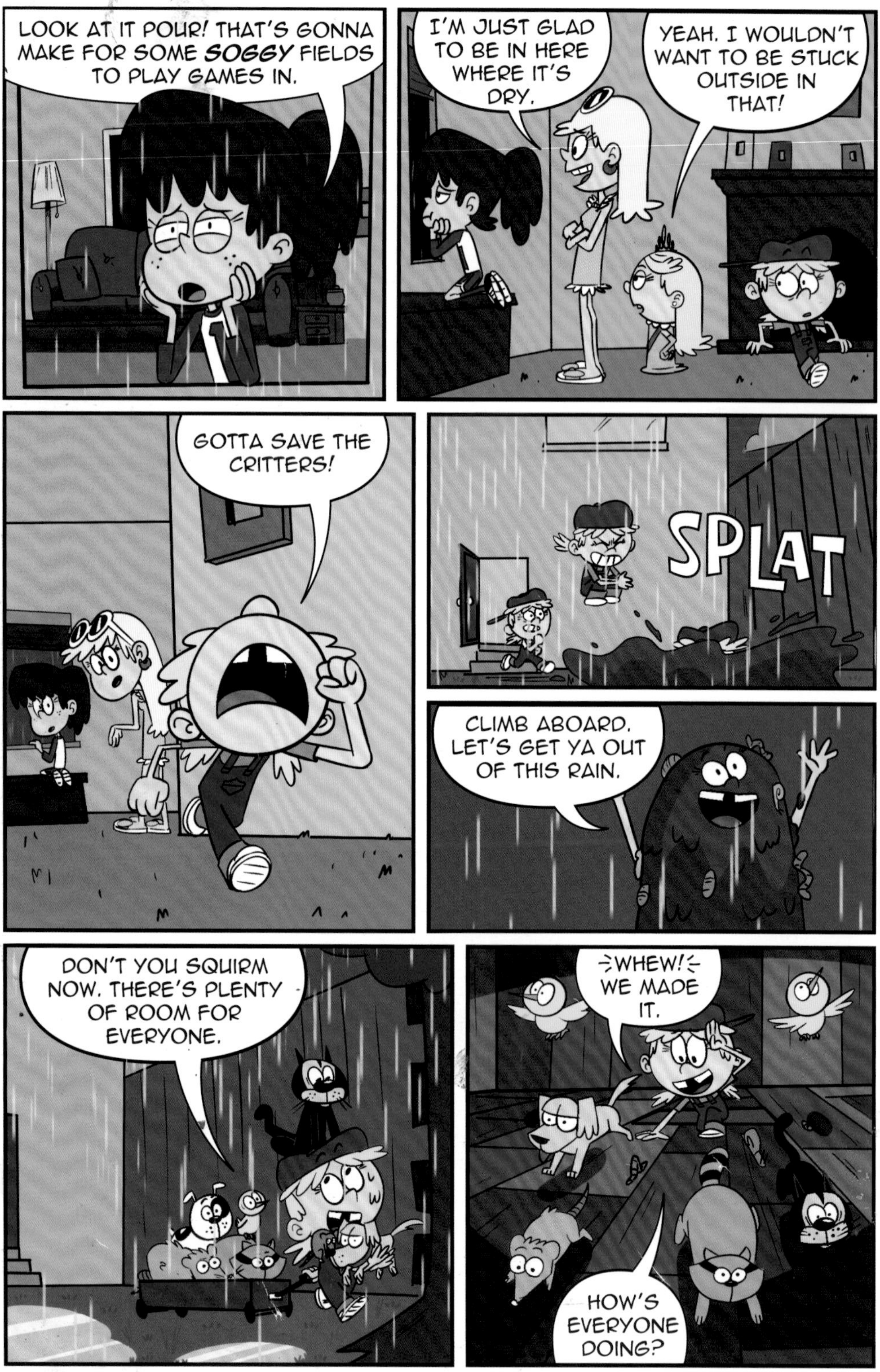

LOOK AT IT POUR! THAT'S GONNA MAKE FOR SOME *SOGGY* FIELDS TO PLAY GAMES IN.
I'M JUST GLAD TO BE IN HERE WHERE IT'S DRY.
YEAH. I WOULDN'T WANT TO BE STUCK OUTSIDE IN THAT!
GOTTA SAVE THE CRITTERS!
SPLAT
CLIMB ABOARD. LET'S GET YA OUT OF THIS RAIN.
DON'T YOU SQUIRM NOW. THERE'S PLENTY OF ROOM FOR EVERYONE.
WHEW! WE MADE IT.
HOW'S EVERYONE DOING?

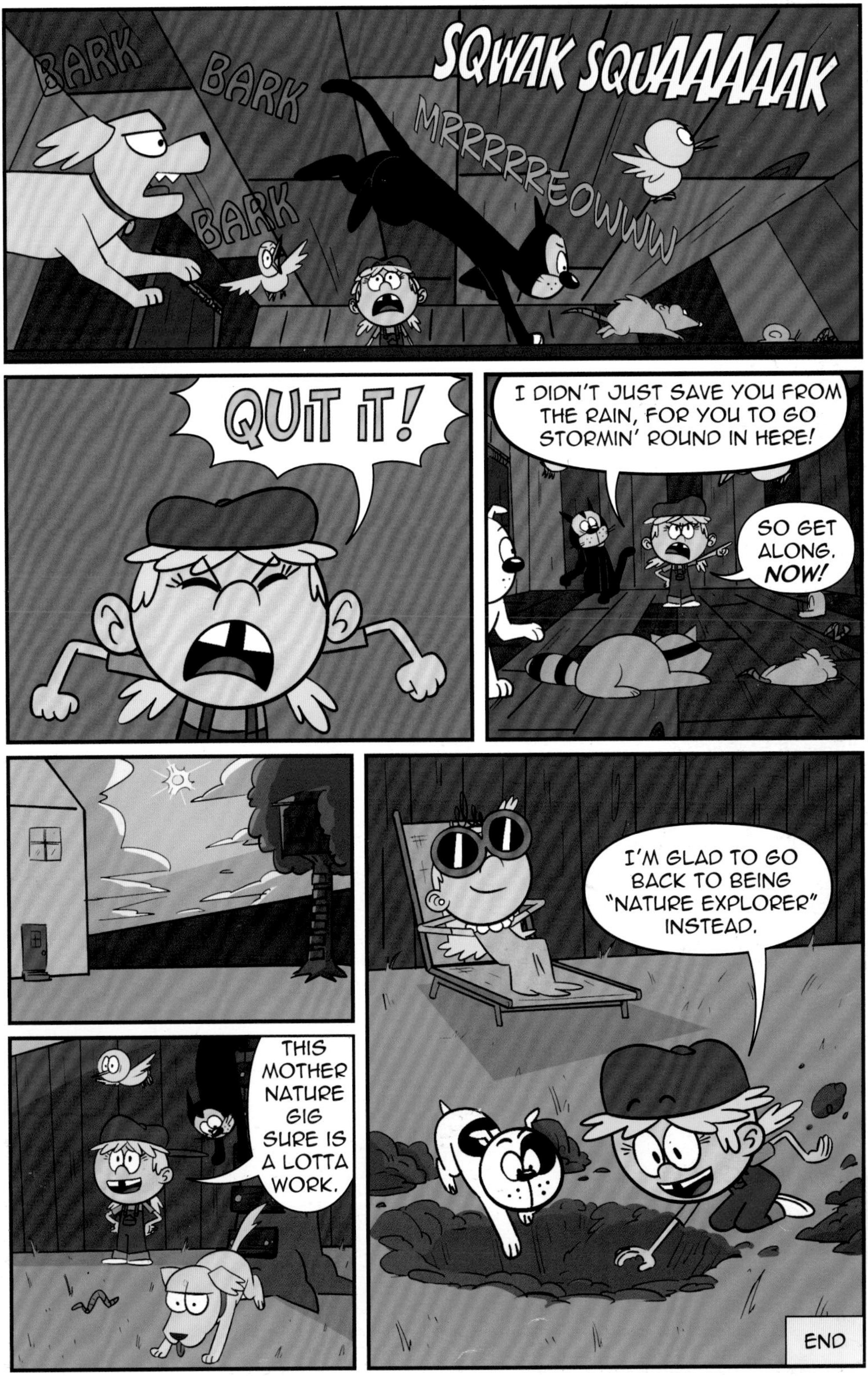
BARK
BARK
BARK
SQWAK SQUAAAAAAK
MRRRRREOWWW
QUIT IT!
I DIDN'T JUST SAVE YOU FROM THE RAIN, FOR YOU TO GO STORMIN' ROUND IN HERE!
SO GET ALONG. NOW!
THIS MOTHER NATURE GIG SURE IS A LOTTA WORK.
I'M GLAD TO GO BACK TO BEING "NATURE EXPLORER" INSTEAD.
END

"A DIRTY RESCUE"

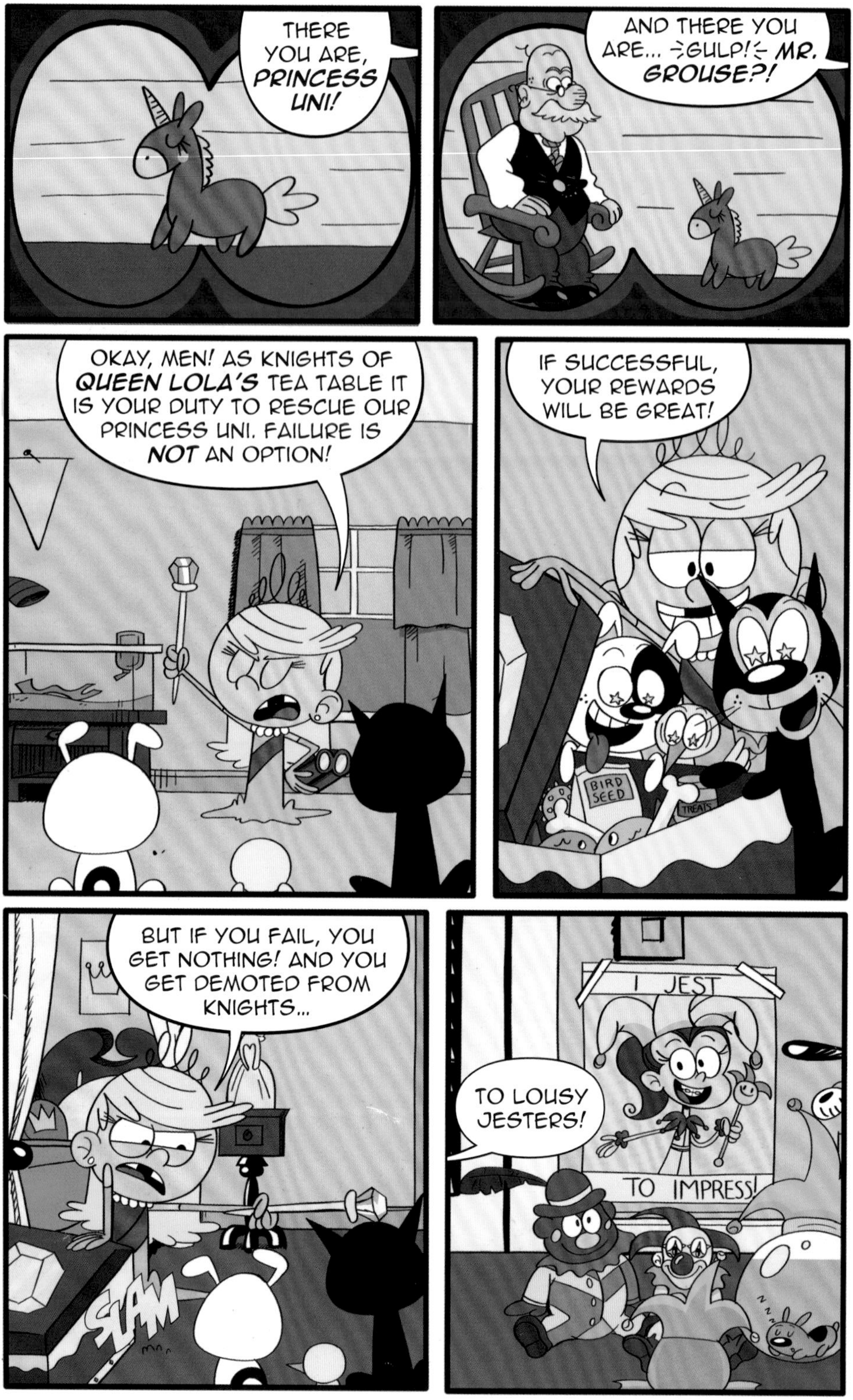

THERE YOU ARE, PRINCESS UNI!
AND THERE YOU ARE... ⇉GULP!⇇ MR. GROUSE?!
OKAY, MEN! AS KNIGHTS OF QUEEN LOLA'S TEA TABLE IT IS YOUR DUTY TO RESCUE OUR PRINCESS UNI. FAILURE IS NOT AN OPTION!
IF SUCCESSFUL, YOUR REWARDS WILL BE GREAT!
BIRD SEED
TREATS
BUT IF YOU FAIL, YOU GET NOTHING! AND YOU GET DEMOTED FROM KNIGHTS...
SLAM
I JEST TO IMPRESS!
TO LOUSY JESTERS!

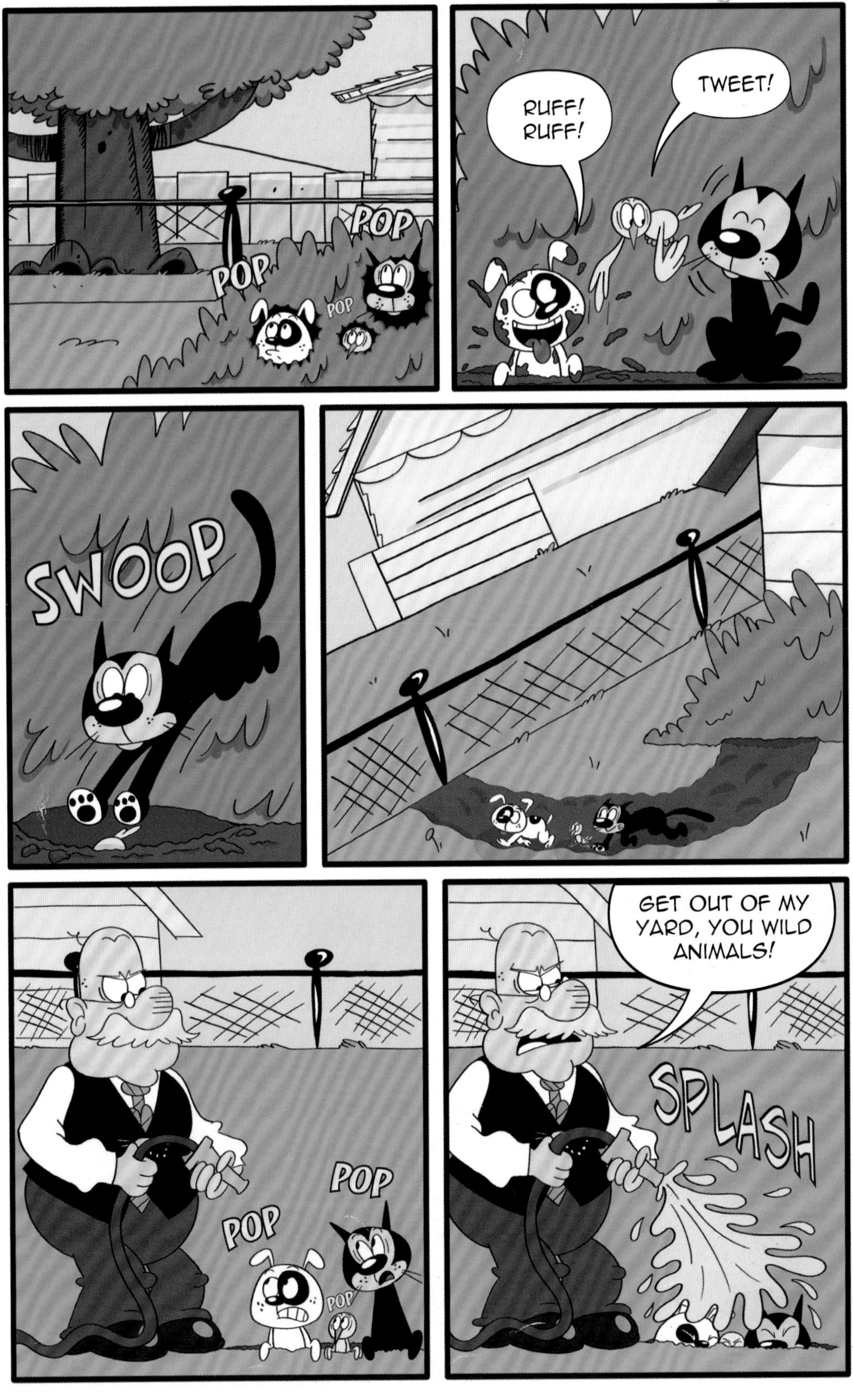
POP
POP
POP
RUFF!
RUFF!
TWEET!
SWOOP
POP
POP
POP
GET OUT OF MY YARD, YOU WILD ANIMALS!
SPLASH

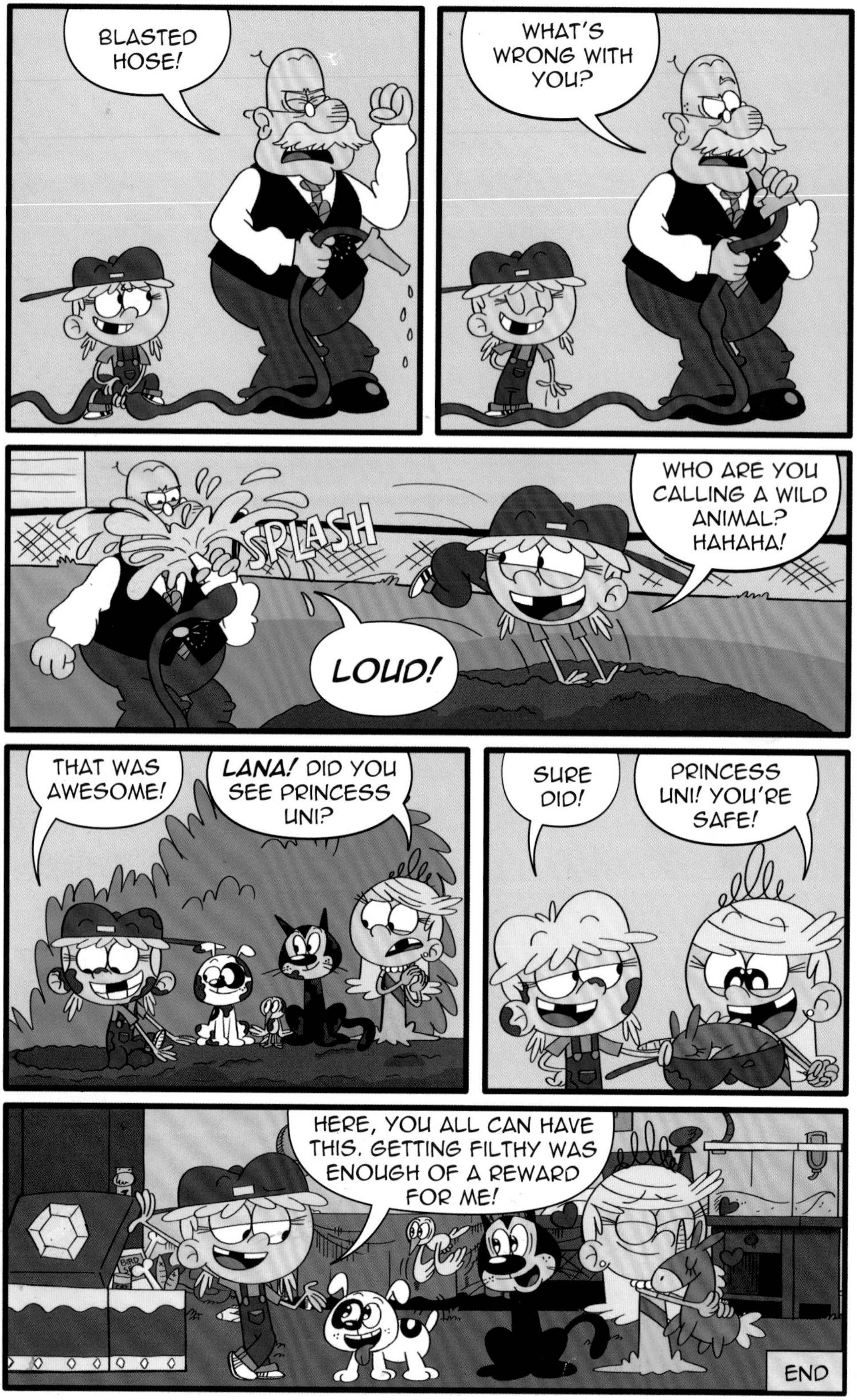
BLASTED HOSE!
WHAT'S WRONG WITH YOU?
SPLASH
WHO ARE YOU CALLING A WILD ANIMAL? HAHAHA!
LOUD!
THAT WAS AWESOME!
LANA! DID YOU SEE PRINCESS UNI?
SURE DID!
PRINCESS UNI! YOU'RE SAFE!
HERE, YOU ALL CAN HAVE THIS. GETTING FILTHY WAS ENOUGH OF A REWARD FOR ME!
END

"FAN FRENZY"

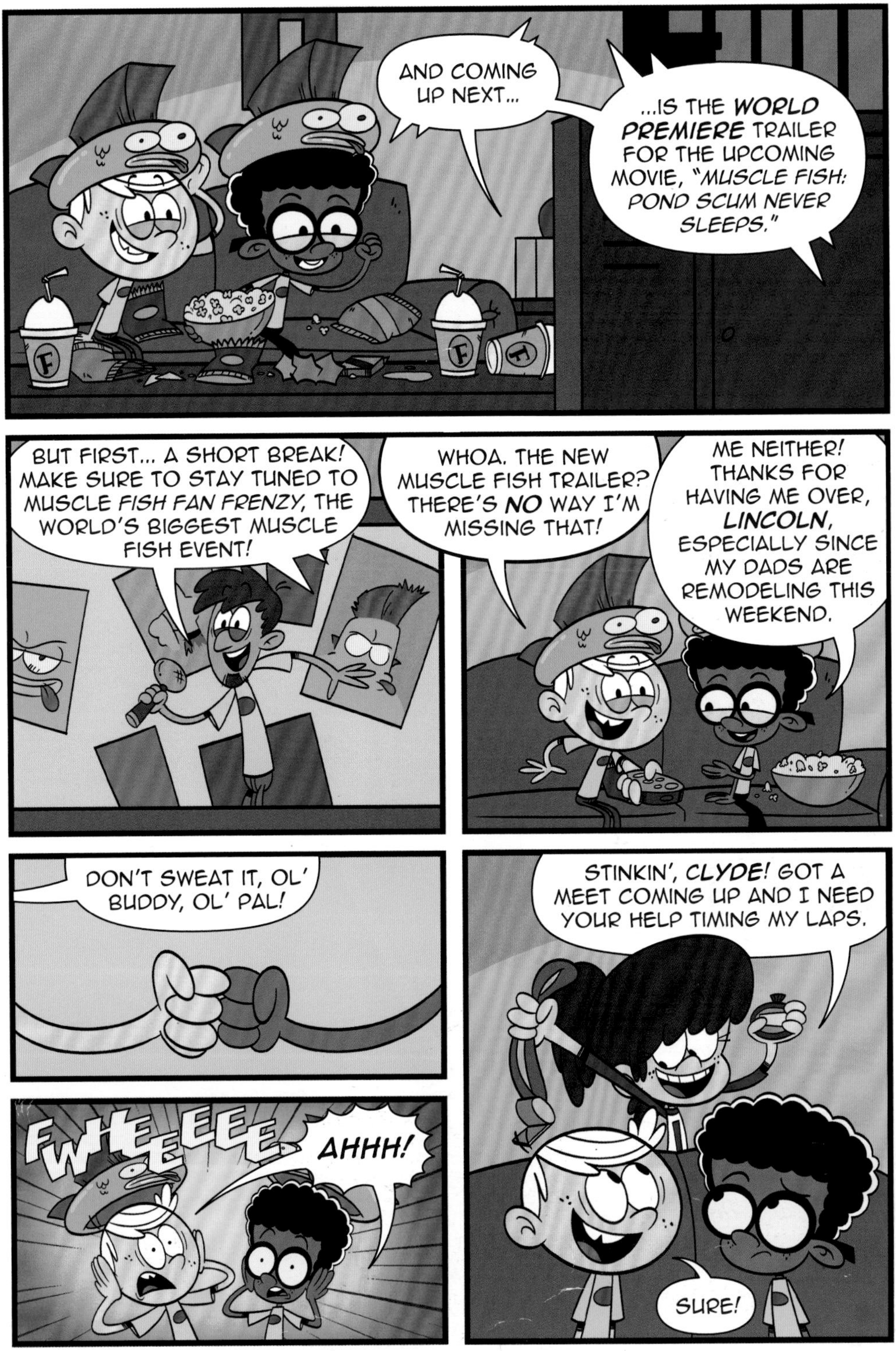

AND COMING UP NEXT...
...IS THE WORLD PREMIERE TRAILER FOR THE UPCOMING MOVIE, "MUSCLE FISH: POND SCUM NEVER SLEEPS."
BUT FIRST... A SHORT BREAK! MAKE SURE TO STAY TUNED TO MUSCLE FISH FAN FRENZY, THE WORLD'S BIGGEST MUSCLE FISH EVENT!
WHOA. THE NEW MUSCLE FISH TRAILER? THERE'S NO WAY I'M MISSING THAT!
ME NEITHER! THANKS FOR HAVING ME OVER, LINCOLN, ESPECIALLY SINCE MY DADS ARE REMODELING THIS WEEKEND.
DON'T SWEAT IT, OL' BUDDY, OL' PAL!
FWHEEEEEE
AHHH!
STINKIN', CLYDE! GOT A MEET COMING UP AND I NEED YOUR HELP TIMING MY LAPS.
SURE!

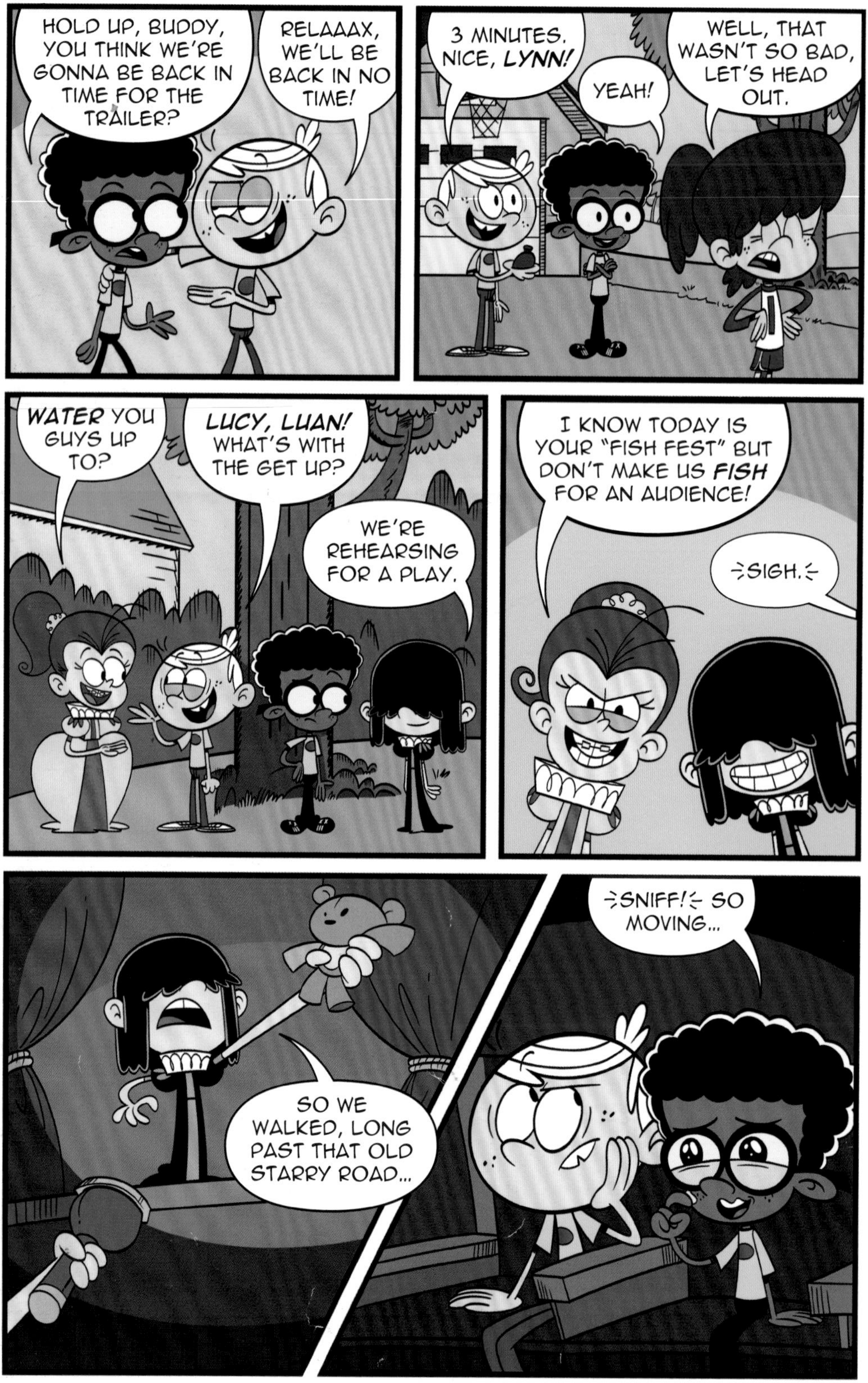
HOLD UP, BUDDY, YOU THINK WE'RE GONNA BE BACK IN TIME FOR THE TRAILER?
RELAAAX, WE'LL BE BACK IN NO TIME!
3 MINUTES. NICE, LYNN!
YEAH!
WELL, THAT WASN'T SO BAD, LET'S HEAD OUT.
WATER YOU GUYS UP TO?
LUCY, LUAN! WHAT'S WITH THE GET UP?
WE'RE REHEARSING FOR A PLAY.
I KNOW TODAY IS YOUR "FISH FEST" BUT DON'T MAKE US FISH FOR AN AUDIENCE!
SIGH.
SO WE WALKED, LONG PAST THAT OLD STARRY ROAD...
SNIFF! SO MOVING...

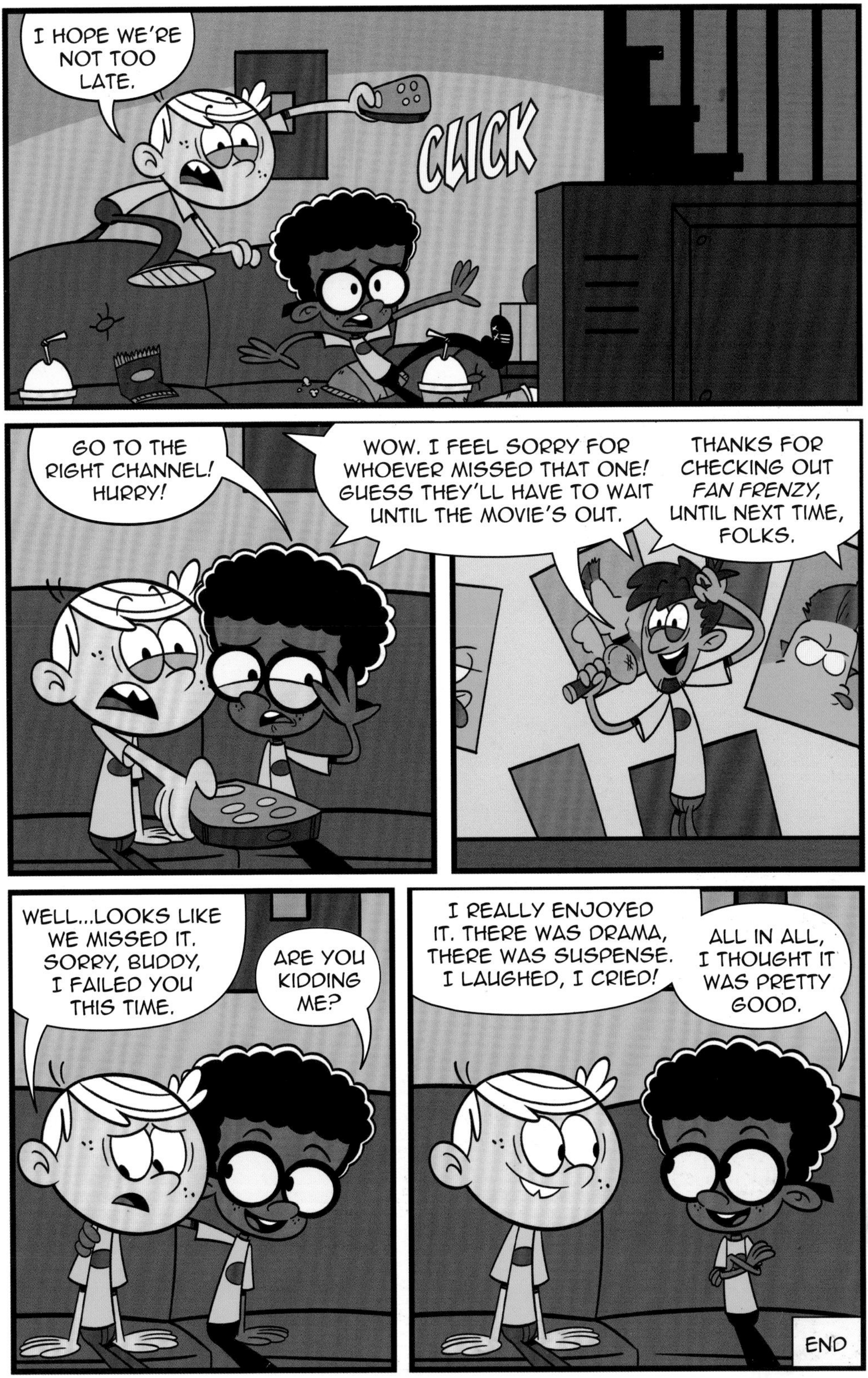
I HOPE WE'RE NOT TOO LATE.
CLICK
GO TO THE RIGHT CHANNEL! HURRY!
WOW. I FEEL SORRY FOR WHOEVER MISSED THAT ONE! GUESS THEY'LL HAVE TO WAIT UNTIL THE MOVIE'S OUT.
THANKS FOR CHECKING OUT *FAN FRENZY*, UNTIL NEXT TIME, FOLKS.
WELL...LOOKS LIKE WE MISSED IT. SORRY, BUDDY, I FAILED YOU THIS TIME.
ARE YOU KIDDING ME?
I REALLY ENJOYED IT. THERE WAS DRAMA, THERE WAS SUSPENSE. I LAUGHED, I CRIED!
ALL IN ALL, I THOUGHT IT WAS PRETTY GOOD.
END

"LISA'S PAPER VIEW"

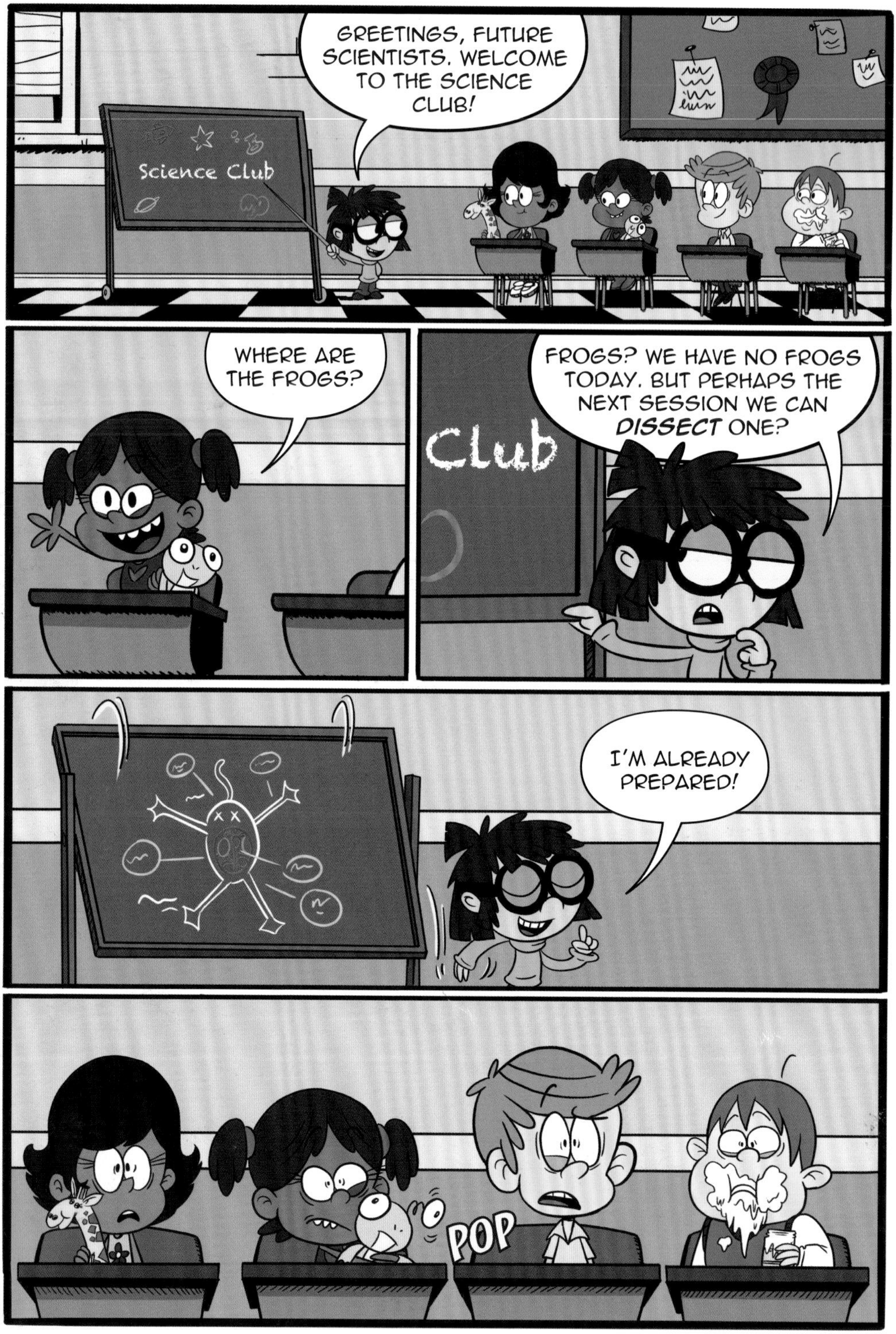
GREETINGS, FUTURE SCIENTISTS. WELCOME TO THE SCIENCE CLUB!
Science Club
WHERE ARE THE FROGS?
Club
FROGS? WE HAVE NO FROGS TODAY. BUT PERHAPS THE NEXT SESSION WE CAN *DISSECT* ONE?
I'M ALREADY PREPARED!
POP

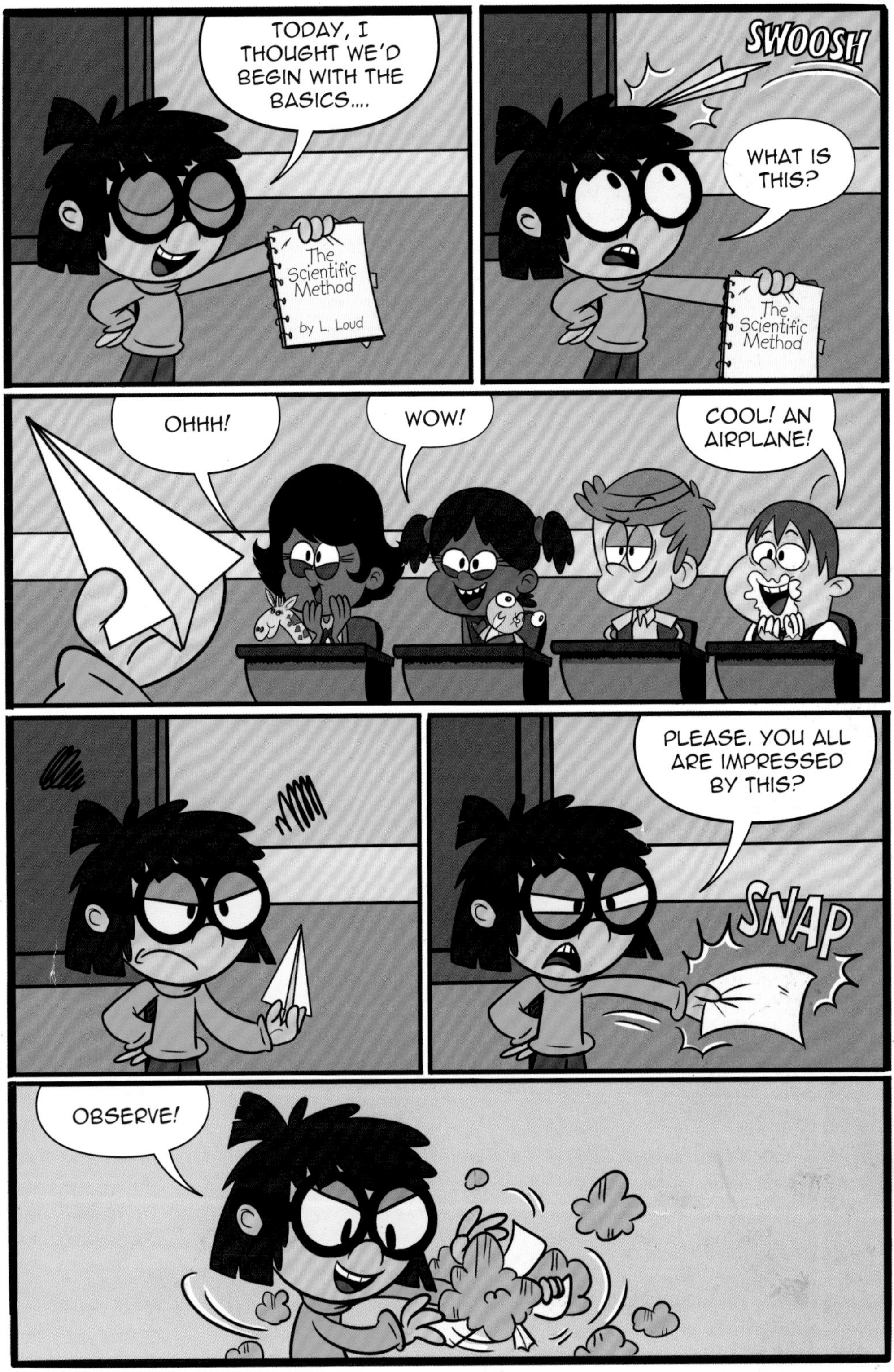
TODAY, I THOUGHT WE'D BEGIN WITH THE BASICS....
The Scientific Method
by L. Loud
SWOOSH
WHAT IS THIS?
The Scientific Method
OHHH!
WOW!
COOL! AN AIRPLANE!
PLEASE. YOU ALL ARE IMPRESSED BY THIS?
SNAP
OBSERVE!

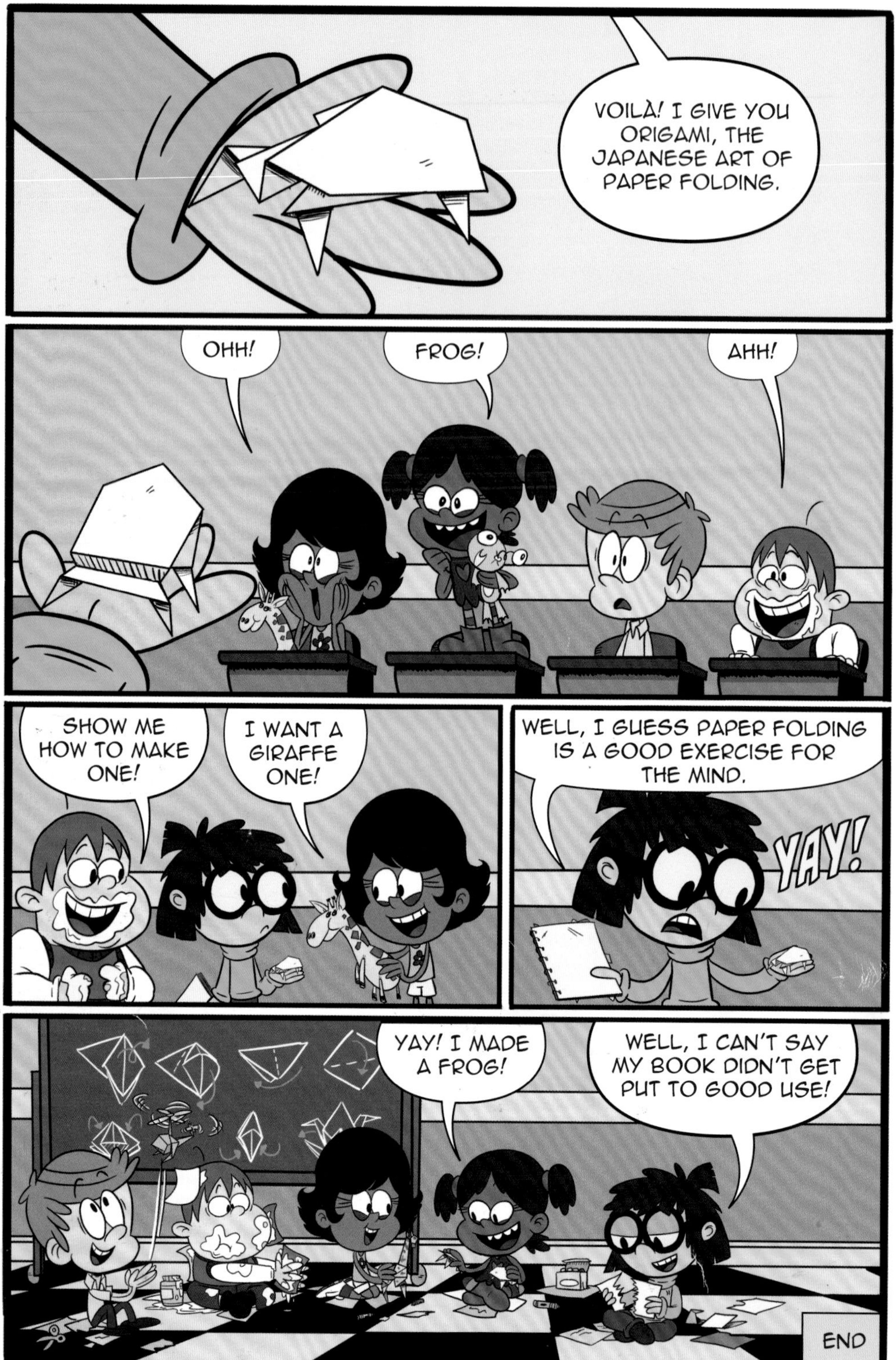
VOILÀ! I GIVE YOU ORIGAMI, THE JAPANESE ART OF PAPER FOLDING.
OHH!
FROG!
AHH!
SHOW ME HOW TO MAKE ONE!
I WANT A GIRAFFE ONE!
WELL, I GUESS PAPER FOLDING IS A GOOD EXERCISE FOR THE MIND.
YAY!
YAY! I MADE A FROG!
WELL, I CAN'T SAY MY BOOK DIDN'T GET PUT TO GOOD USE!
END

"CLOSING MIME"

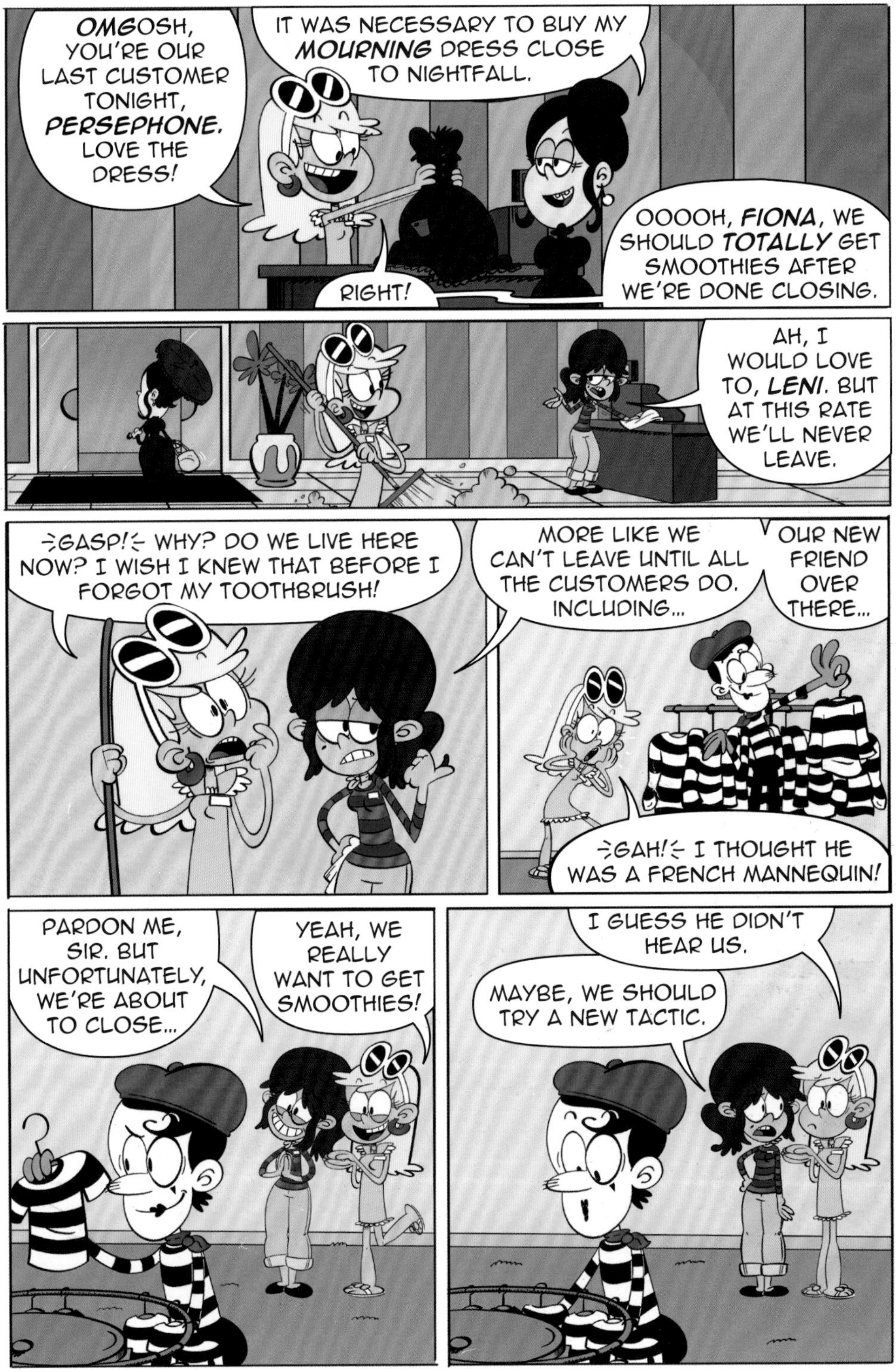
OMGOSH, YOU'RE OUR LAST CUSTOMER TONIGHT, PERSEPHONE. LOVE THE DRESS!
IT WAS NECESSARY TO BUY MY MOURNING DRESS CLOSE TO NIGHTFALL.
RIGHT!
OOOOH, FIONA, WE SHOULD TOTALLY GET SMOOTHIES AFTER WE'RE DONE CLOSING.
AH, I WOULD LOVE TO, LENI. BUT AT THIS RATE WE'LL NEVER LEAVE.
GASP! WHY? DO WE LIVE HERE NOW? I WISH I KNEW THAT BEFORE I FORGOT MY TOOTHBRUSH!
MORE LIKE WE CAN'T LEAVE UNTIL ALL THE CUSTOMERS DO. INCLUDING...
OUR NEW FRIEND OVER THERE...
GAH! I THOUGHT HE WAS A FRENCH MANNEQUIN!
PARDON ME, SIR. BUT UNFORTUNATELY, WE'RE ABOUT TO CLOSE...
YEAH, WE REALLY WANT TO GET SMOOTHIES!
I GUESS HE DIDN'T HEAR US.
MAYBE, WE SHOULD TRY A NEW TACTIC.

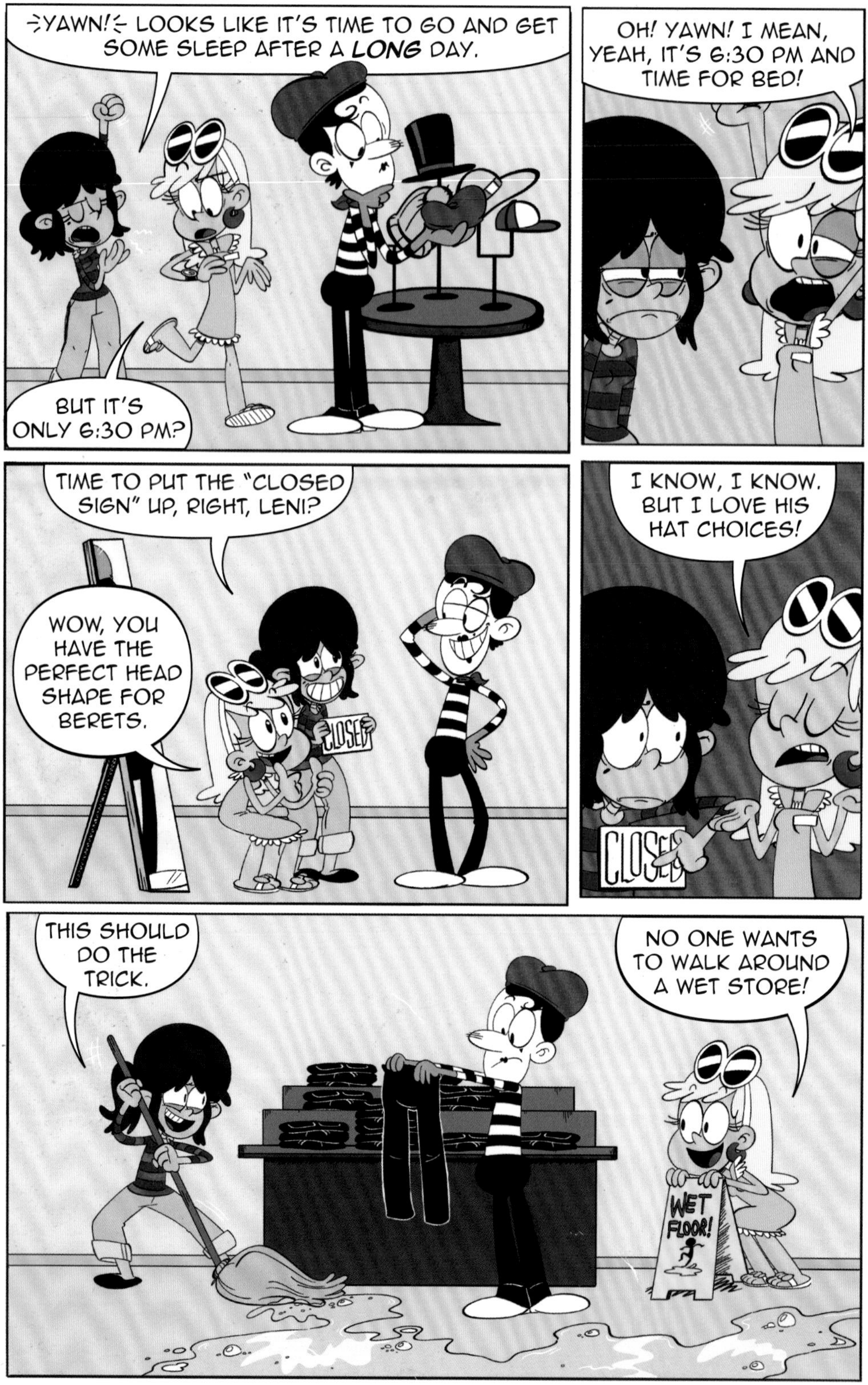

⇒YAWN!⇐ LOOKS LIKE IT'S TIME TO GO AND GET SOME SLEEP AFTER A **LONG** DAY.
BUT IT'S ONLY 6:30 PM?
OH! YAWN! I MEAN, YEAH, IT'S 6:30 PM AND TIME FOR BED!
TIME TO PUT THE "CLOSED SIGN" UP, RIGHT, LENI?
WOW, YOU HAVE THE PERFECT HEAD SHAPE FOR BERETS.
CLOSED
I KNOW, I KNOW. BUT I LOVE HIS HAT CHOICES!
CLOSED
THIS SHOULD DO THE TRICK.
NO ONE WANTS TO WALK AROUND A WET STORE!
WET FLOOR!

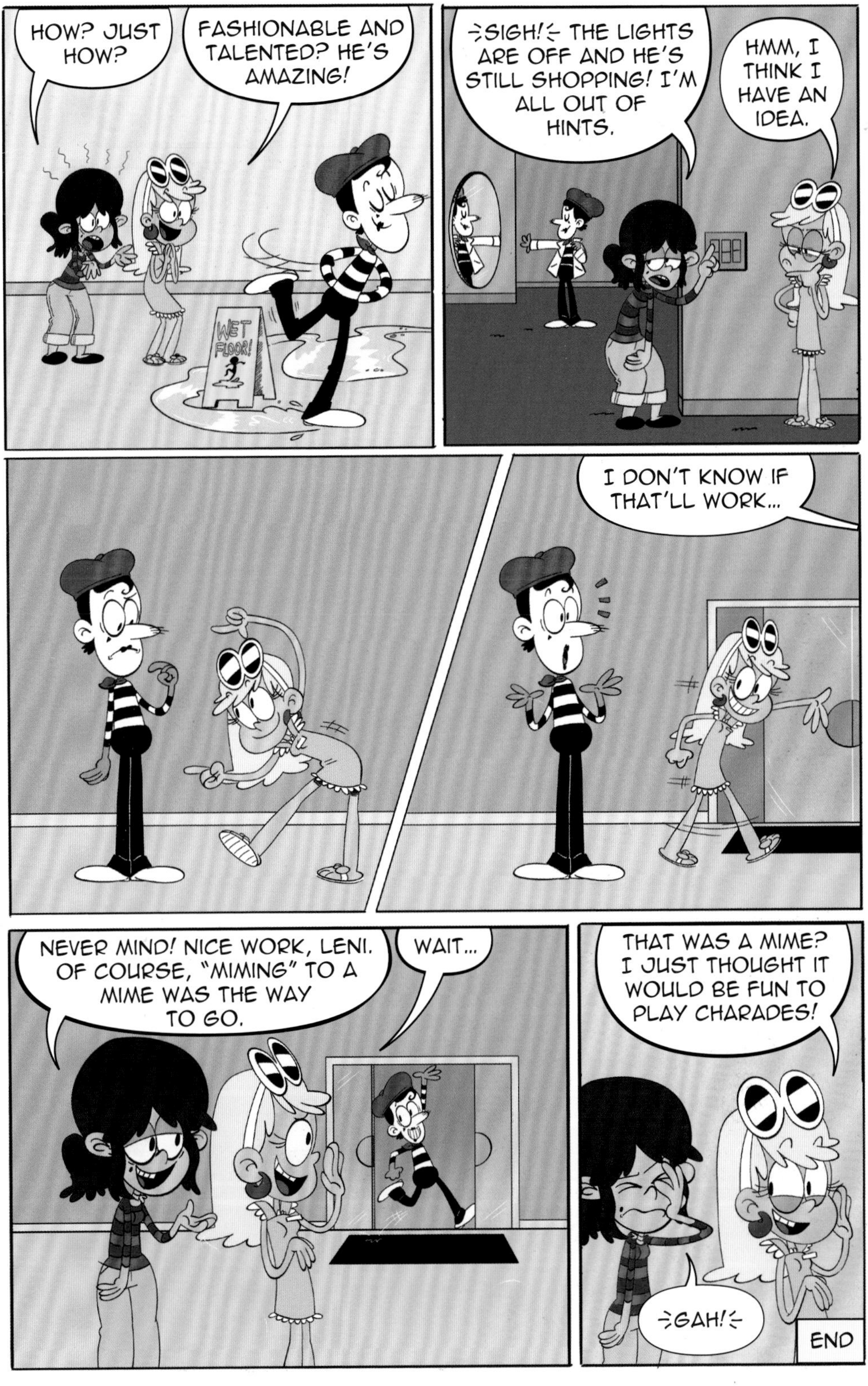
HOW? JUST HOW?
FASHIONABLE AND TALENTED? HE'S AMAZING!
WET FLOOR!
⇒SIGH!⇐ THE LIGHTS ARE OFF AND HE'S STILL SHOPPING! I'M ALL OUT OF HINTS.
HMM, I THINK I HAVE AN IDEA.
I DON'T KNOW IF THAT'LL WORK...
NEVER MIND! NICE WORK, LENI. OF COURSE, "MIMING" TO A MIME WAS THE WAY TO GO.
WAIT...
THAT WAS A MIME? I JUST THOUGHT IT WOULD BE FUN TO PLAY CHARADES!
⇒GAH!⇐
END

"GONE GNOME"

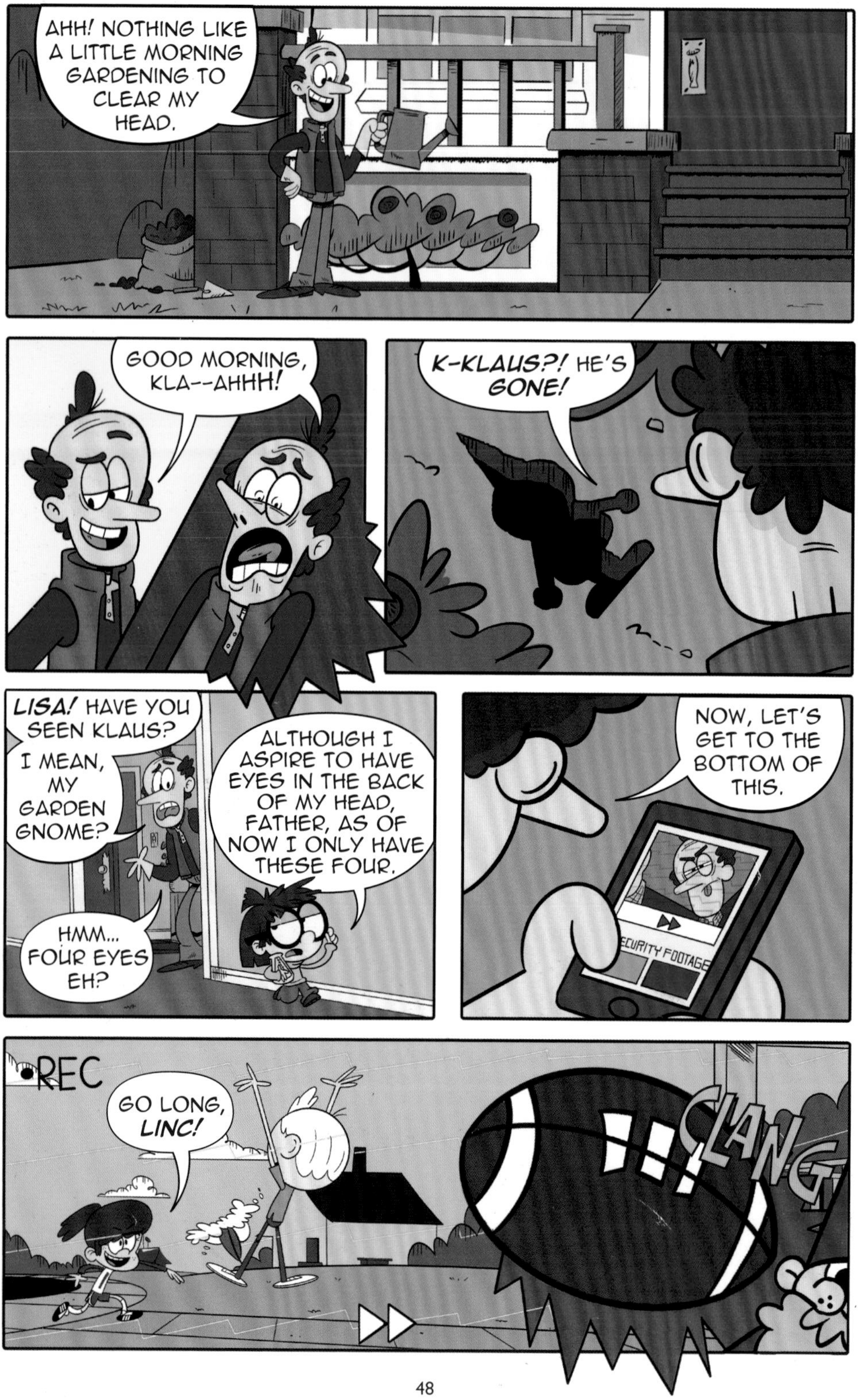
AHH! NOTHING LIKE A LITTLE MORNING GARDENING TO CLEAR MY HEAD.
GOOD MORNING, KLA--AHHH!
K-KLAUS?! HE'S GONE!
LISA! HAVE YOU SEEN KLAUS?
I MEAN, MY GARDEN GNOME?
ALTHOUGH I ASPIRE TO HAVE EYES IN THE BACK OF MY HEAD, FATHER, AS OF NOW I ONLY HAVE THESE FOUR.
HMM... FOUR EYES EH?
NOW, LET'S GET TO THE BOTTOM OF THIS.
SECURITY FOOTAGE
•REC
GO LONG, LINC!
CLANG!

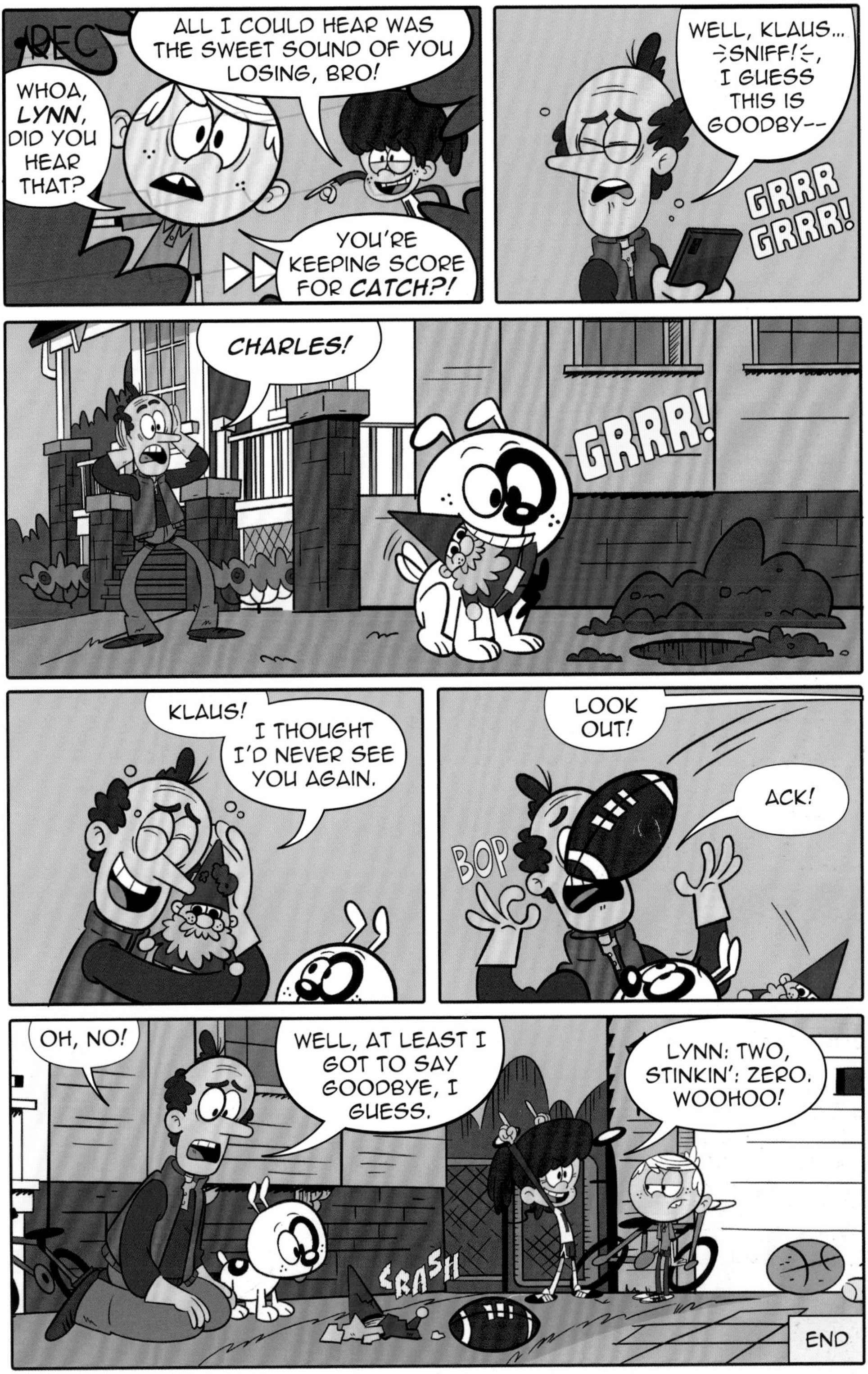
REC
WHOA, LYNN, DID YOU HEAR THAT?
ALL I COULD HEAR WAS THE SWEET SOUND OF YOU LOSING, BRO!
YOU'RE KEEPING SCORE FOR CATCH?!
WELL, KLAUS... SNIFF!, I GUESS THIS IS GOODBY--
GRRR GRRR!
CHARLES!
GRRR!
KLAUS! I THOUGHT I'D NEVER SEE YOU AGAIN.
LOOK OUT!
ACK!
BOP
OH, NO!
WELL, AT LEAST I GOT TO SAY GOODBYE, I GUESS.
LYNN: TWO, STINKIN': ZERO. WOOHOO!
CRASH
END

"FRIENDS FUR-EVER"

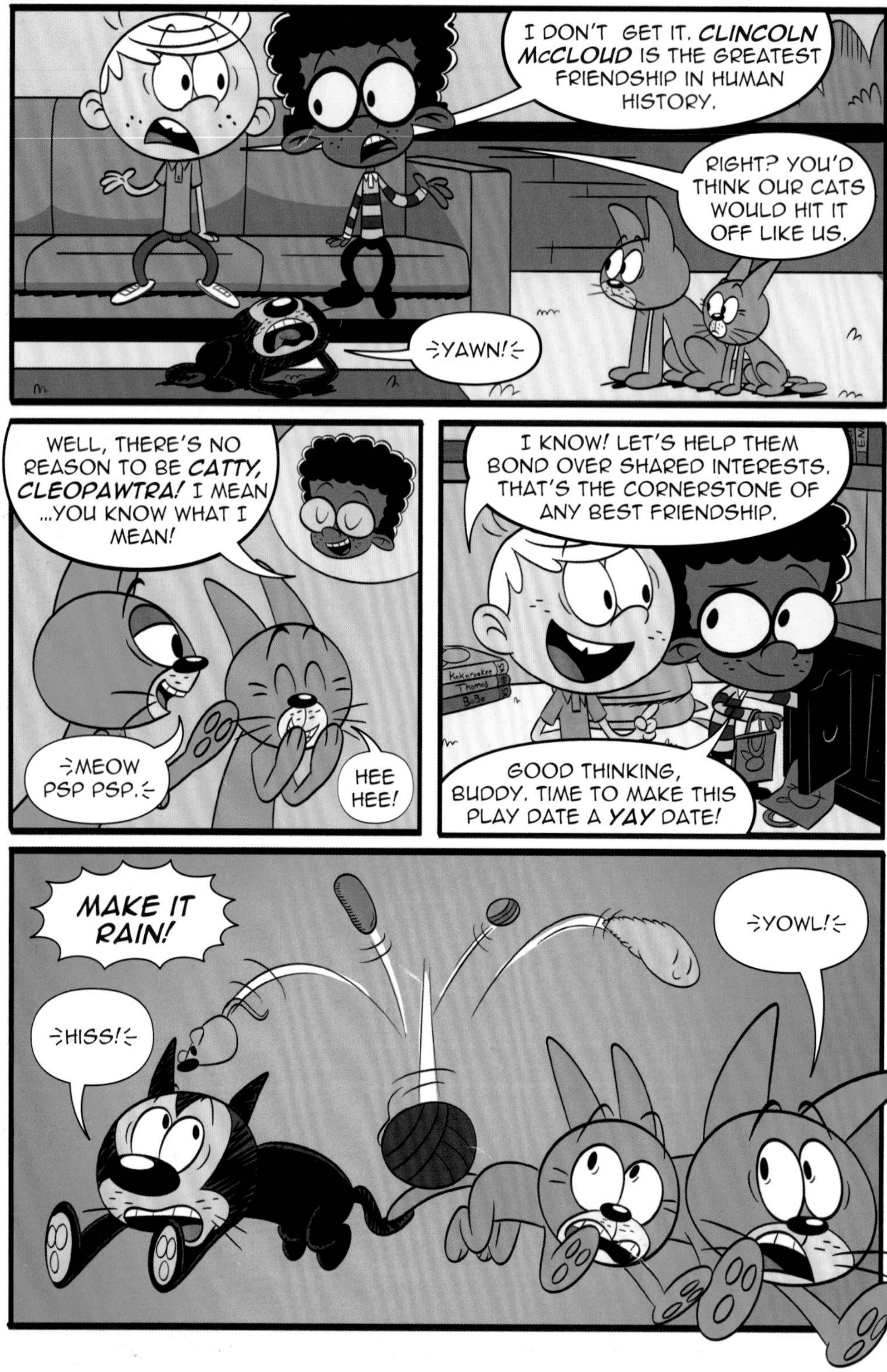

I DON'T GET IT. CLINCOLN McCLOUD IS THE GREATEST FRIENDSHIP IN HUMAN HISTORY.
RIGHT? YOU'D THINK OUR CATS WOULD HIT IT OFF LIKE US.
YAWN!
WELL, THERE'S NO REASON TO BE CATTY, CLEOPAWTRA! I MEAN ...YOU KNOW WHAT I MEAN!
MEOW PSP PSP.
HEE HEE!
I KNOW! LET'S HELP THEM BOND OVER SHARED INTERESTS. THAT'S THE CORNERSTONE OF ANY BEST FRIENDSHIP.
GOOD THINKING, BUDDY. TIME TO MAKE THIS PLAY DATE A YAY DATE!
MAKE IT RAIN!
YOWL!
HISS!

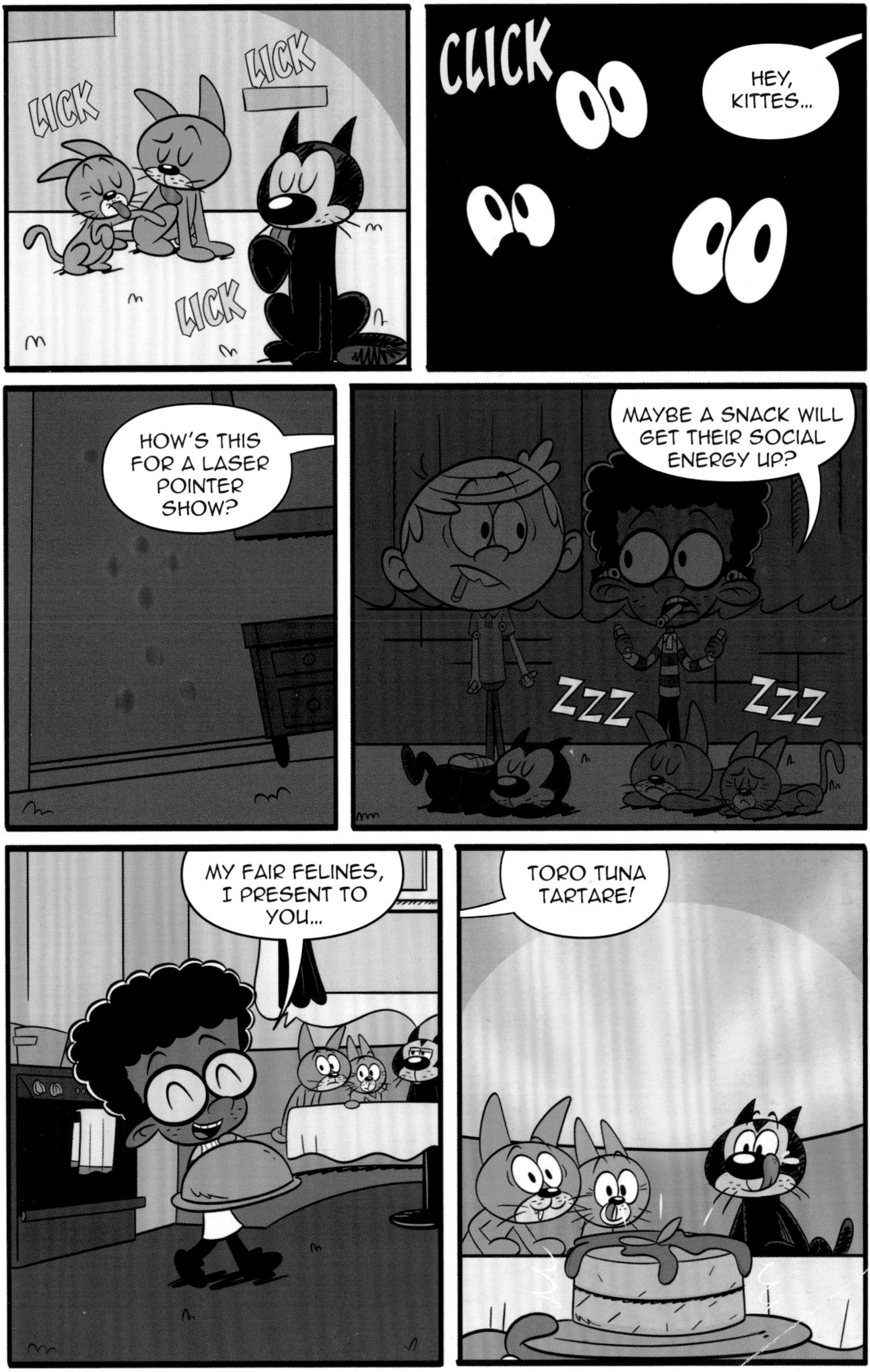
LICK
LICK
LICK
CLICK
HEY, KITTES...
HOW'S THIS FOR A LASER POINTER SHOW?
MAYBE A SNACK WILL GET THEIR SOCIAL ENERGY UP?
ZZZ
ZZZ
MY FAIR FELINES, I PRESENT TO YOU...
TORO TUNA TARTARE!

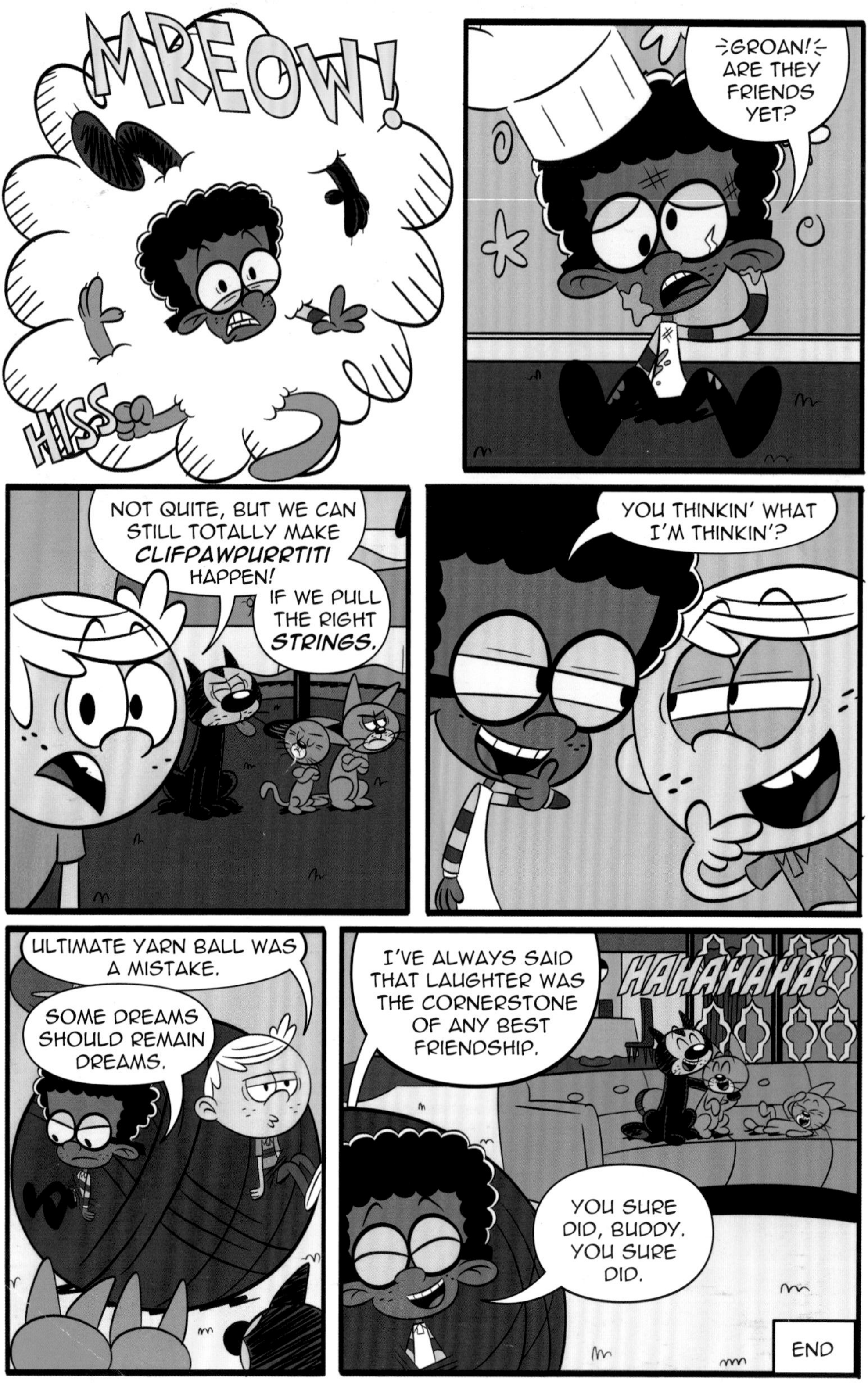
MREOW!
HISS
GROAN!
ARE THEY FRIENDS YET?
NOT QUITE, BUT WE CAN STILL TOTALLY MAKE CLIFPAWPURRTITI HAPPEN!
IF WE PULL THE RIGHT STRINGS.
YOU THINKIN' WHAT I'M THINKIN'?
ULTIMATE YARN BALL WAS A MISTAKE.
SOME DREAMS SHOULD REMAIN DREAMS.
I'VE ALWAYS SAID THAT LAUGHTER WAS THE CORNERSTONE OF ANY BEST FRIENDSHIP.
HAHAHAHA!
YOU SURE DID, BUDDY. YOU SURE DID.
END

"PURRSONAL HYGIENE"

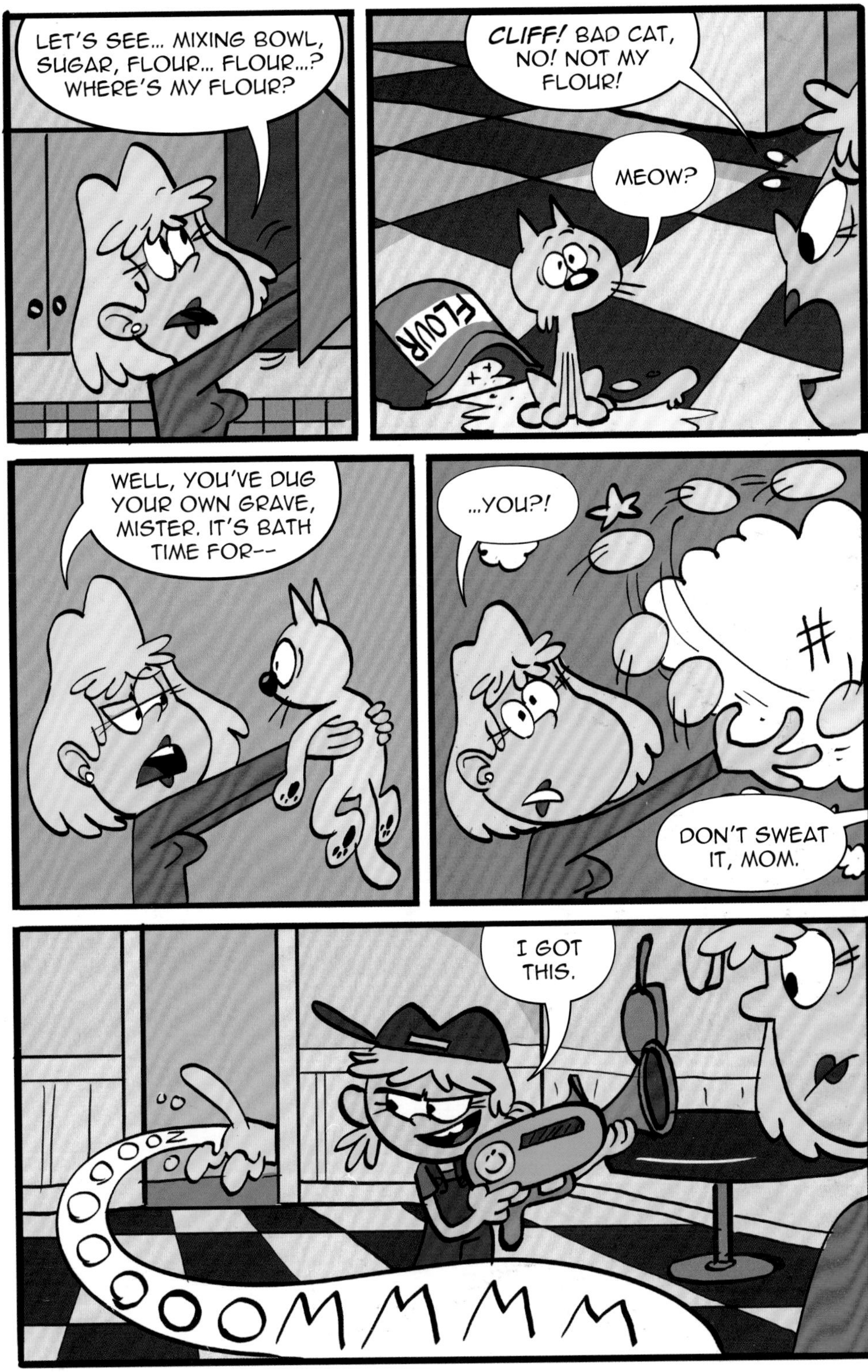
LET'S SEE... MIXING BOWL, SUGAR, FLOUR... FLOUR...? WHERE'S MY FLOUR?
CLIFF! BAD CAT, NO! NOT MY FLOUR!
MEOW?
FLOUR
WELL, YOU'VE DUG YOUR OWN GRAVE, MISTER. IT'S BATH TIME FOR--
...YOU?!
DON'T SWEAT IT, MOM.
I GOT THIS.
OOZ
OOOOOOOMMMMM

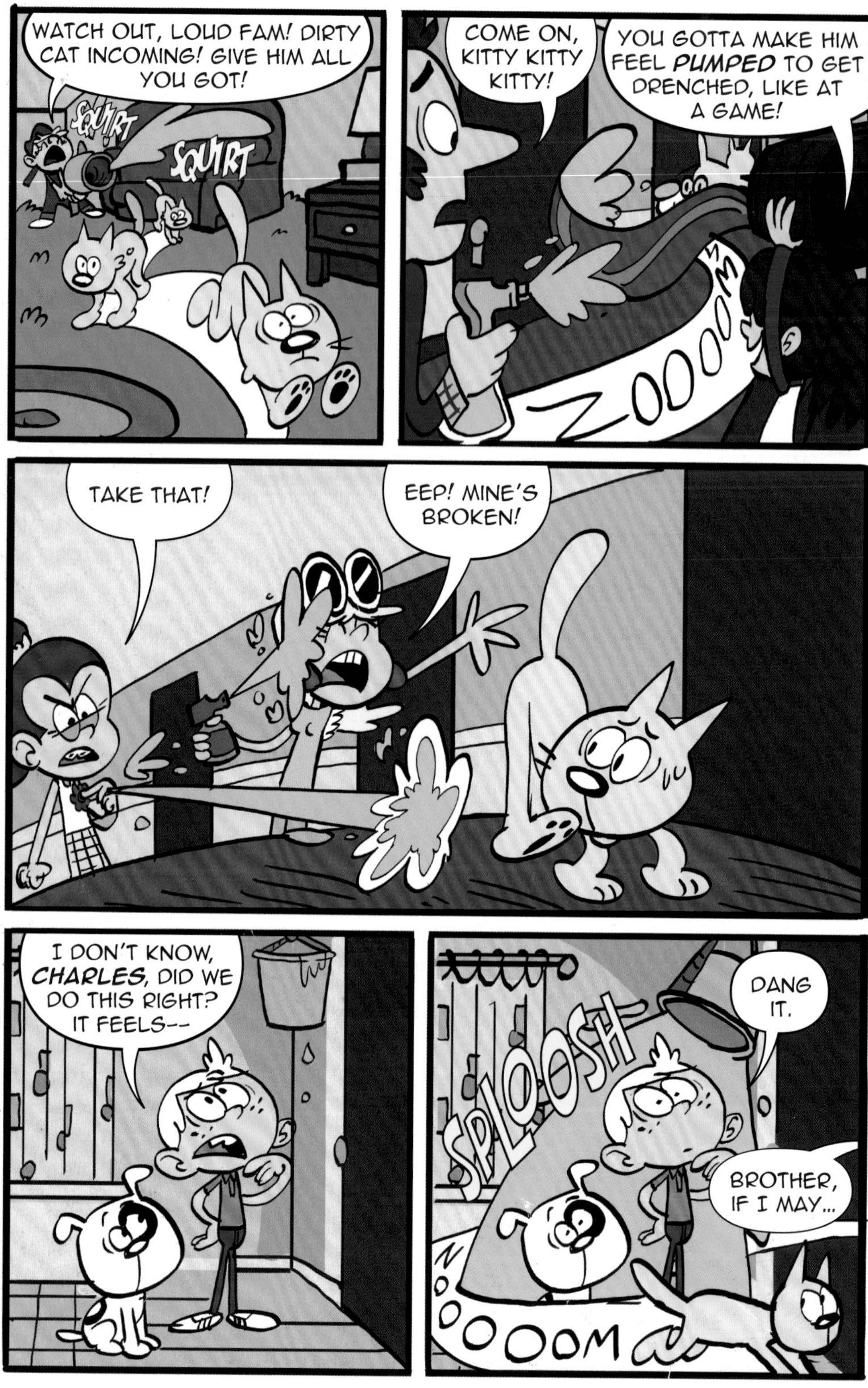
WATCH OUT, LOUD FAM! DIRTY CAT INCOMING! GIVE HIM ALL YOU GOT!
SQUIRT
SQUIRT
COME ON, KITTY KITTY KITTY!
YOU GOTTA MAKE HIM FEEL PUMPED TO GET DRENCHED, LIKE AT A GAME!
ZOOOOOM
TAKE THAT!
EEP! MINE'S BROKEN!
I DON'T KNOW, CHARLES, DID WE DO THIS RIGHT? IT FEELS--
SPLOOSH
DANG IT.
BROTHER, IF I MAY...
NOOOOOM

THERE'S NO WAY YOU'LL BE ABLE TO BATHE THE CAT THAT EASILY... IT'S PART OF THE LIQUID-TO-CAT VARIABLE. NO MATTER HOW DIRTY THE CAT, THEY WILL ALWAYS REJECT LIQUID.

A FOUNDATI FELIS CATU

FACTOIDS & STUDY

UNLESS...

BY ALTERING THE DNA RESPONSIBLE FOR THE UBIQUITOUS LIQUID-TO-CAT VARIABLE, IT'S POSSIBLE TO MAKE A CAT TOLERATE WATER- OR EVEN BETTER, LEARN TO ENJOY IT. ALL WE NEED TO DO IS A SIMPLE PROC... ...A SIMPLE MA... ...GRAME. IT SH... ...N A PINCH. ...ER OF ...WI... ...IN THE AMY... ...ITHOUT F... ...CUP

OR, IN OTHER WORDS, JUST USE MY NEW MACHINE, THE AMYGDALA CHURNER! A TOTALLY ANIMAL TESTED AND EFFECTIVE WAY TO MAKE CATS NATURALLY HYDROPHILIC.

UHH... *LISA*, ARE YOU SURE THAT'S, Y'KNOW, SAFE?

MY DEAR, DEAR SIBLING, HAVE I EVER DONE YOU WRONG?

WELL--

IN JUST A MOMENT, YOU'LL SEE JUST HOW EFFECTIVE THIS WILL BE!

LET'S FIND THAT DIRTY CAT, AND--

WHAT! CLIFF CLEANED HIMSELF?!

HAH, I GUESS WE WON'T NEED TO USE YOUR MACHINE AFTER ALL!

SLURP

YES, I SUPPOSE WE WON'T...

THIS TIME...

END

"ONE GOOD PUSH"

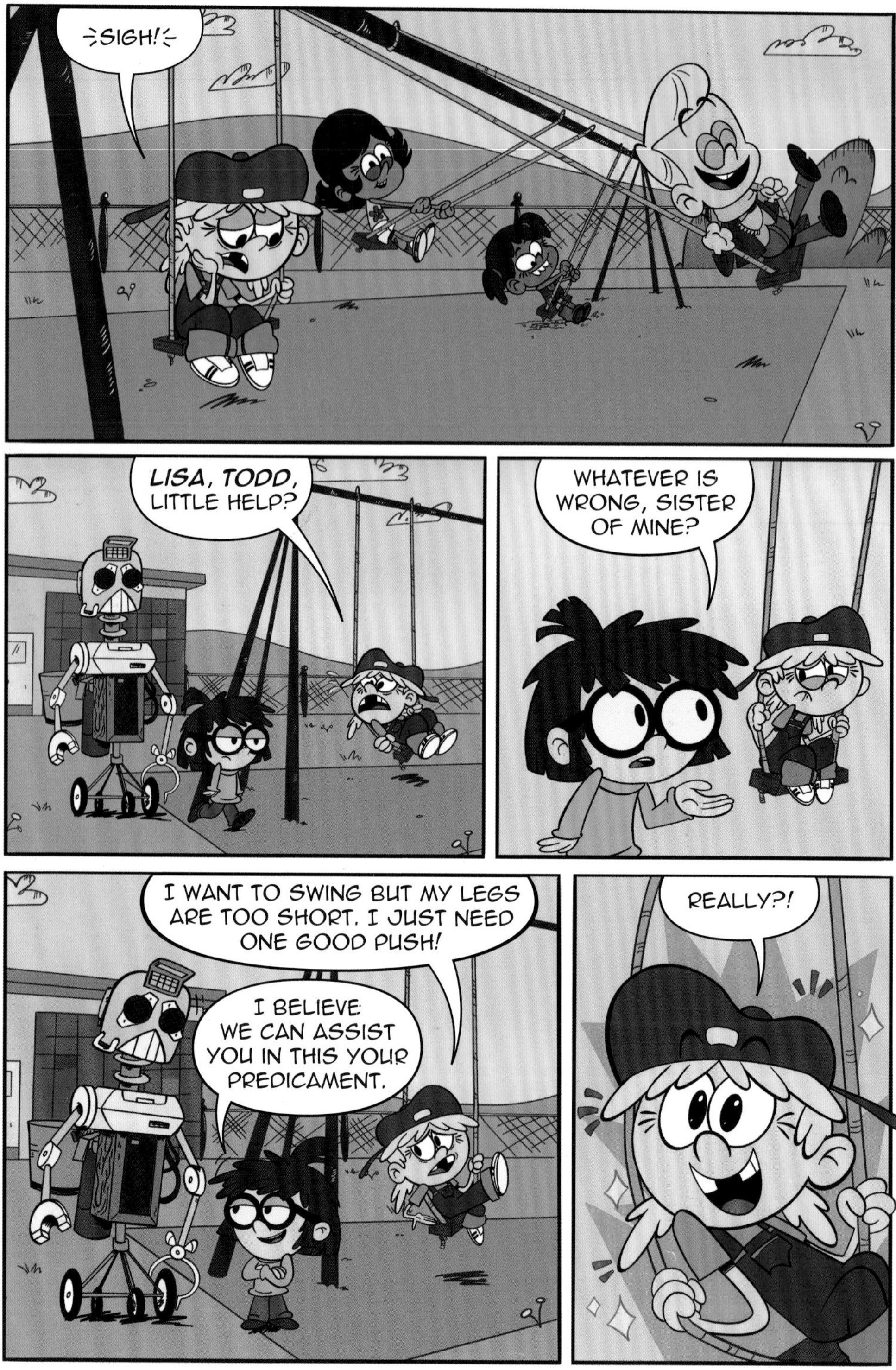
SIGH!
LISA, TODD, LITTLE HELP?
WHATEVER IS WRONG, SISTER OF MINE?
I WANT TO SWING BUT MY LEGS ARE TOO SHORT. I JUST NEED ONE GOOD PUSH!
I BELIEVE WE CAN ASSIST YOU IN THIS YOUR PREDICAMENT.
REALLY?!

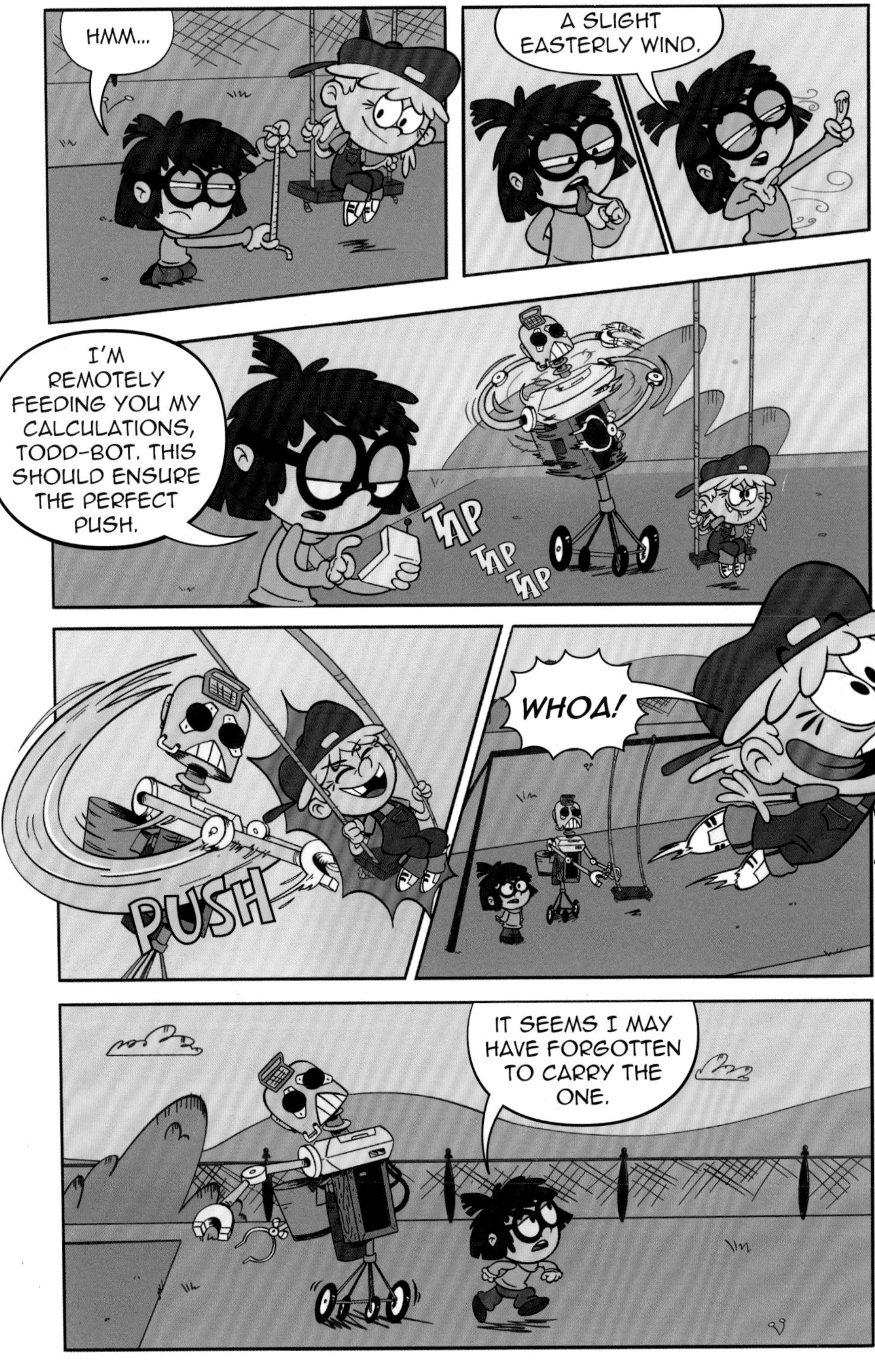
HMM...
A SLIGHT EASTERLY WIND.
I'M REMOTELY FEEDING YOU MY CALCULATIONS, TODD-BOT. THIS SHOULD ENSURE THE PERFECT PUSH.
TAP
TAP
TAP
PUSH
WHOA!
IT SEEMS I MAY HAVE FORGOTTEN TO CARRY THE ONE.

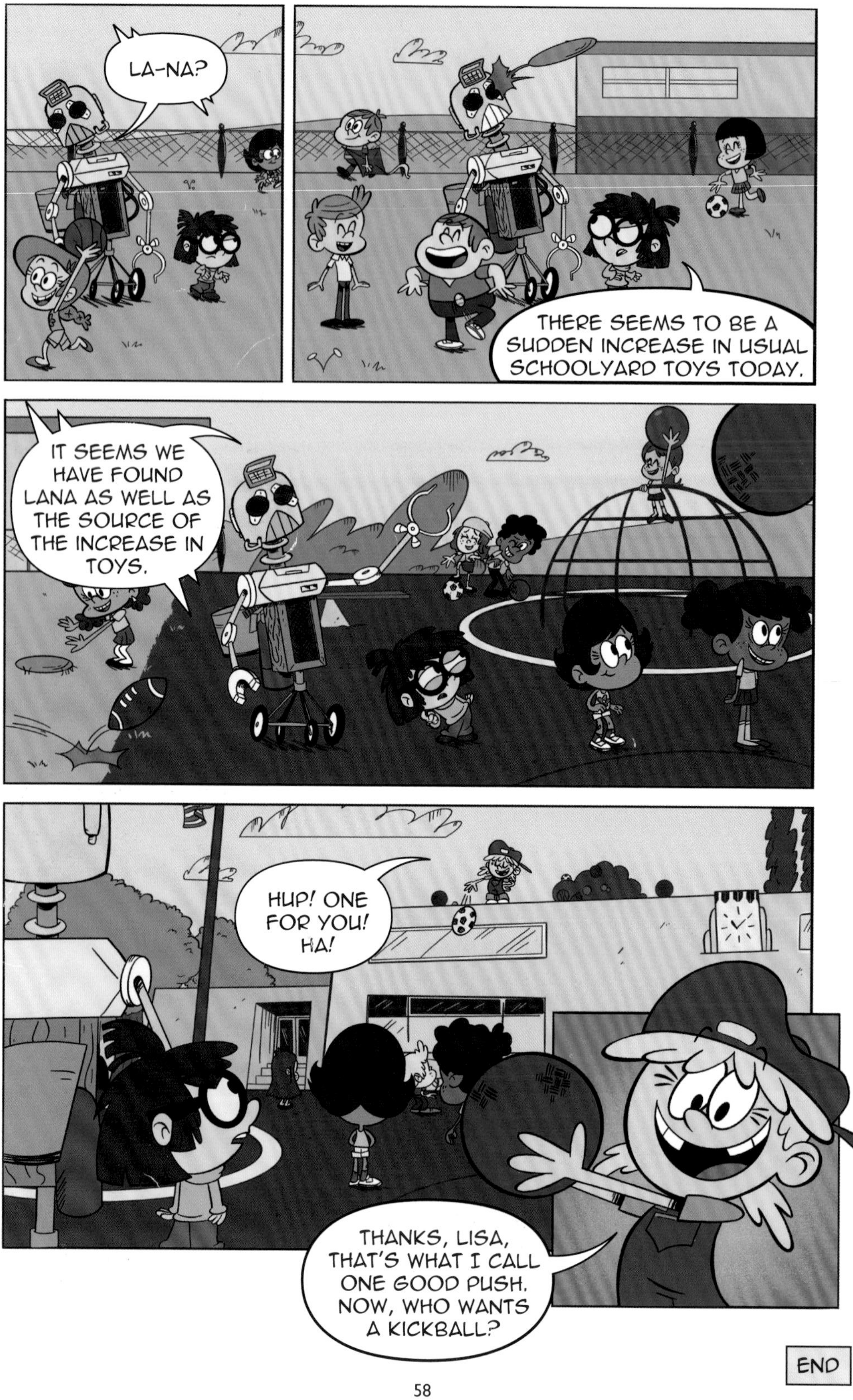
LA-NA?
THERE SEEMS TO BE A SUDDEN INCREASE IN USUAL SCHOOLYARD TOYS TODAY.
IT SEEMS WE HAVE FOUND LANA AS WELL AS THE SOURCE OF THE INCREASE IN TOYS.
HUP! ONE FOR YOU! HA!
THANKS, LISA, THAT'S WHAT I CALL ONE GOOD PUSH. NOW, WHO WANTS A KICKBALL?
END

WATCH OUT FOR PAPERCUTZ™

Welcome to the fifteenth family-member-finding THE LOUD HOUSE graphic novel "The Missing Linc." It's from Papercutz, those never-lost souls dedicated to publishing great graphic novels for all ages. I'm Jim Salicrup, Editor-in-Chief and Former Lost Boy, here to search for another Papercutz series you may enjoy—that you should be able to easily find at your favorite bookseller or library.

So let me tell you about THE SMURFS TALES by Peyo. If you've been enjoying the all-new Smurfs animated series on Nickelodeon, it's a safe bet you'll love the comics that inspired the cartoons. That's right, unlike THE LOUD HOUSE, which started as an animated TV series on Nickelodeon and then became THE LOUD HOUSE Papercutz graphic novels, THE SMURFS started out as comics first—before becoming a huge success in animated cartoons and movies. And THE SMURFS comics that Papercutz has been publishing are the original comics in which THE SMURFS made their debut.

Now, you may think at first that tiny blue elves living in little mushroom houses have nothing in common with the various members of Lincoln Loud's family, but we beg to differ. For example, both Leni Loud and Vanity Smurf care a lot about fashion—they love to look fabulous! Luna Loud and Harmony Smurf both love making music—Luna's just a lot better at it! Luan Loud and Jokey Smurf both love a good prank! Lynn Loud and Hefty Smurf are both super competitive when it comes to sports! Lola Loud and Smurfette are both natural born queens! Lana Loud and Handy Smurf are both unafraid to get down and dirty and fix anything that's broken! Lisa Loud and Brainy Smurf are both big thinkers, but Lisa is actually as smart as Brainy wishes he was! Lily Loud and Baby Smurf are both—well, babies and super adorable! Hey, even the Loud's grumpy neighbor, Mr. Grouse, is a little like Grouchy Smurf!

Probably the biggest things the Louds and the Smurfs have in common is that they all love each other and have the most amazing fun adventures! In general, even in "the real world," we all tend to have far more in common than it may at first appear. No matter your size, shape, color, or gender, we all are looking for the same things in life. We hope that you

have already found true happiness in your life, but if you haven't, please don't give up! Even if things look hopeless, never give up! Whatever you're searching for may soon be found as easily as a certain "missing" Linc was found.

We also hope you find some joy and happiness in such Papercutz graphic novels as THE SMURFS TALES, THE SMURFS 3 IN 1, THE CASAGRANDES, THE LOUD HOUSE 3 IN1, and of course, right here in THE LOUD HOUSE. As any family member of the Casagrandes would say, *mi casa, su casa*. Or our (Loud) house, is your house. You're welcome here, and we hope you come back again soon for THE LOUD HOUSE #16, "Loud and Clear." (Check out the little sneak preview on page 62!) It won't be as much fun without you!

Thanks, Jim

STAY IN TOUCH!

EMAIL:	salicrup@papercutz.com
WEB:	papercutz.com
TWITTER:	@papercutzgn
INSTAGRAM:	@papercutzgn
FACEBOOK:	PAPERCUTZGRAPHICNOVELS
FANMAIL:	Papercutz, 160 Broadway, Suite 700, East Wing, New York, NY 10038

Go to papercutz.com and sign up for the free Papercutz e-newsletter!

nickelodeon GRAPHIC NOVELS AVAILABLE FROM PAPERCUTZ

THE LOUD HOUSE
THERE WILL BE CHAOS

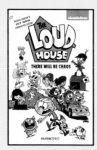

THE LOUD HOUSE
#1
"There Will Be Chaos"

THE LOUD HOUSE

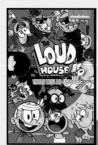

THE LOUD HOUSE
#2
"There Will Be More Chaos"

THE LOUD HOUSE
LIVE LIFE LOUD!

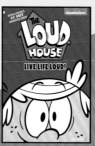

THE LOUD HOUSE
#3
"Live Life Loud!"

THE LOUD HOUSE
FAMILY TREE
KEEP OUT!

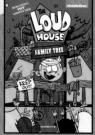

THE LOUD HOUSE
#4
"Family Tree"

THE LOUD HOUSE
AFTER DARK

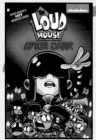

THE LOUD HOUSE
#5
"After Dark"

THE LOUD HOUSE
LOUD & PROUD

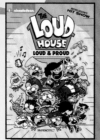

THE LOUD HOUSE
#6
"Loud and Proud"

THE LOUD HOUSE
THE STRUGGLE IS REAL

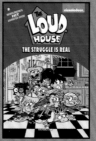

THE LOUD HOUSE
#7
"The Struggle is Real"

THE LOUD HOUSE
Livin' La Casa Loud!

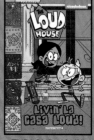

THE LOUD HOUSE
#8
"Livin' La Casa Loud"

THE LOUD HOUSE
ULTIMATE HANGOUT

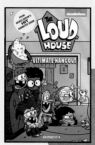

THE LOUD HOUSE
#9
"Ultimate Hangout"

THE LOUD HOUSE
THE MANY FACES OF LINCOLN LOUD

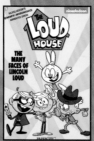

THE LOUD HOUSE
#10
"The Many Faces of Lincoln Loud"

THE LOUD HOUSE
WHO'S THE LOUDEST?

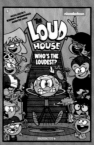

THE LOUD HOUSE
#11
"Who's the Loudest?"

THE LOUD HOUSE
THE CASE OF THE STOLEN DRAWERS

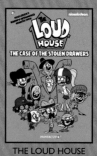

THE LOUD HOUSE
#12
"The Case of the Stolen Drawers"

COMING SOON

THE LOUD HOUSE
LUCY ROLLS THE DICE

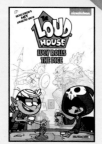

THE LOUD HOUSE
#13
"Lucy Rolls the Dice"

THE LOUD HOUSE
GUESSING GAMES

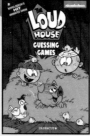

THE LOUD HOUSE
#14
"Guessing Games"

THE LOUD HOUSE
THE MISSING LINC

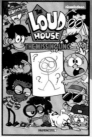

THE LOUD HOUSE
#15
"The Missing Linc"

THE LOUD HOUSE
LOUD AND CLEAR

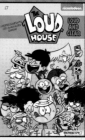

THE LOUD HOUSE
#16
"Loud and Clear"

COMING SOON

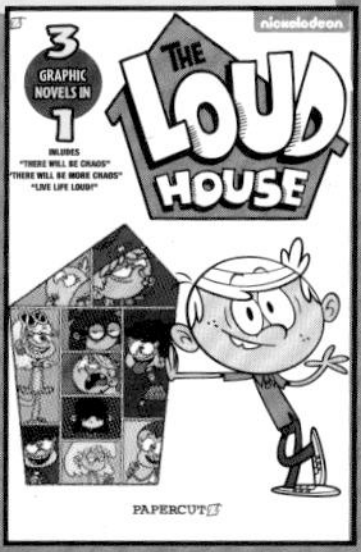

nickelodeon
3 GRAPHIC NOVELS IN 1
THE LOUD HOUSE
PAPERCUTZ

THE LOUD HOUSE
3 IN 1
#1

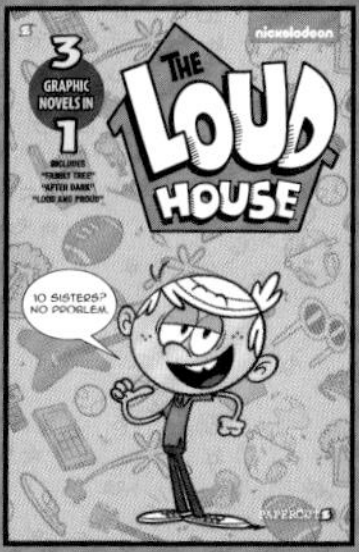

nickelodeon
3 GRAPHIC NOVELS IN 1
THE LOUD HOUSE
10 SISTERS? NO PROBLEM.
PAPERCUTZ

THE LOUD HOUSE
3 IN 1
#2

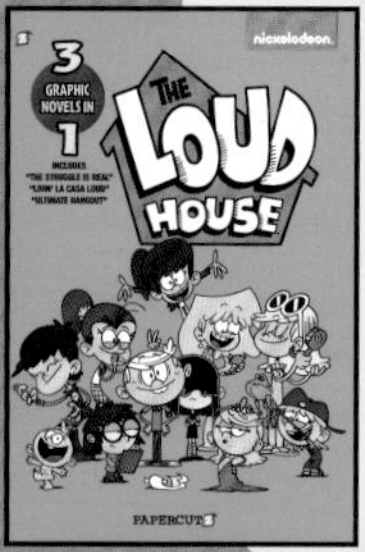

nickelodeon
3 GRAPHIC NOVELS IN 1
THE LOUD HOUSE
PAPERCUTZ

THE LOUD HOUSE
3 IN 1
#3

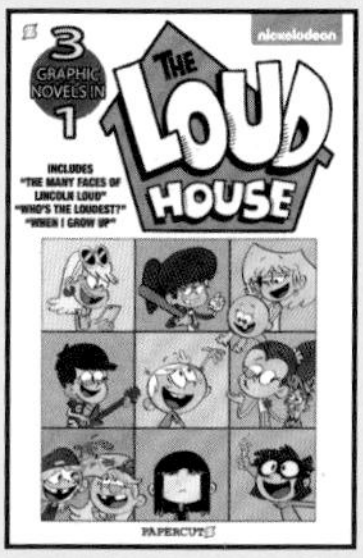

nickelodeon
3 GRAPHIC NOVELS IN 1
THE LOUD HOUSE
PAPERCUTZ

THE LOUD HOUSE
3 IN 1
#4

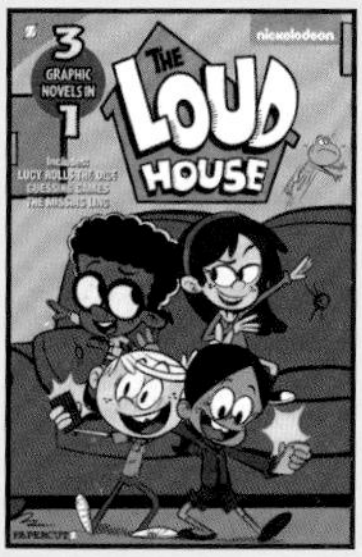

nickelodeon
3 GRAPHIC NOVELS IN 1
THE LOUD HOUSE

THE LOUD HOUSE
3 IN 1
#5

COMING SOON

COMING SOON

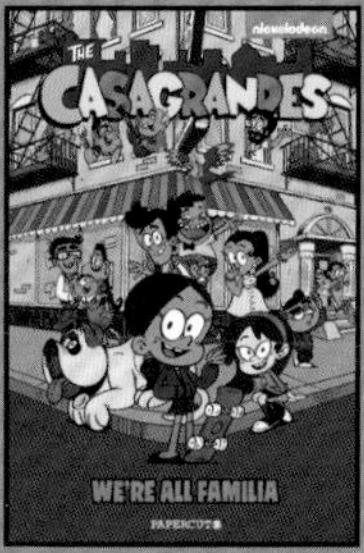

nickelodeon
THE CASAGRANDES
WE'RE ALL FAMILIA
PAPERCUTZ

THE CASAGRANDES
#1
"We're All Familia"

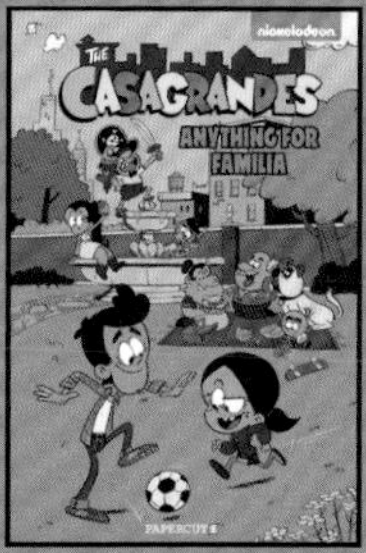

nickelodeon
THE CASAGRANDES
ANYTHING FOR FAMILIA
PAPERCUTZ

THE CASAGRANDES
#2
"Anything for Familia"

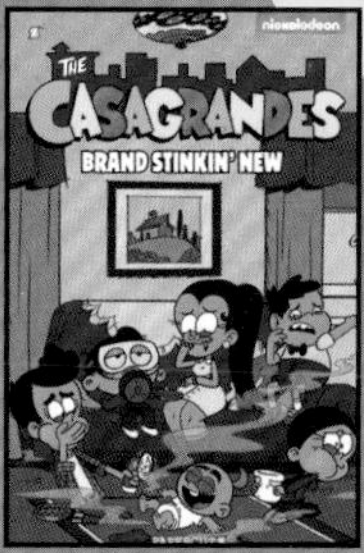

nickelodeon
THE CASAGRANDES
BRAND STINKIN' NEW

THE CASAGRANDES
#3
"Brand Stinkin' New"

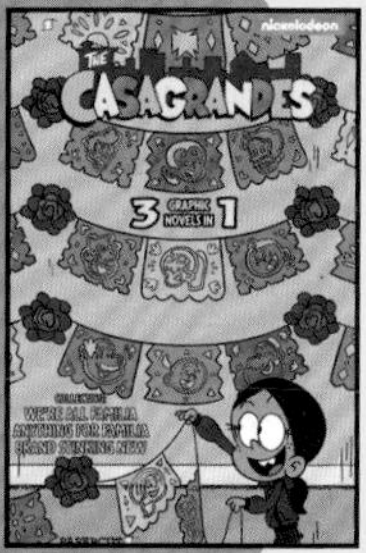

nickelodeon
THE CASAGRANDES
3 GRAPHIC NOVELS IN 1

THE CASAGRANDES
3 IN 1
#1

COMING SOON

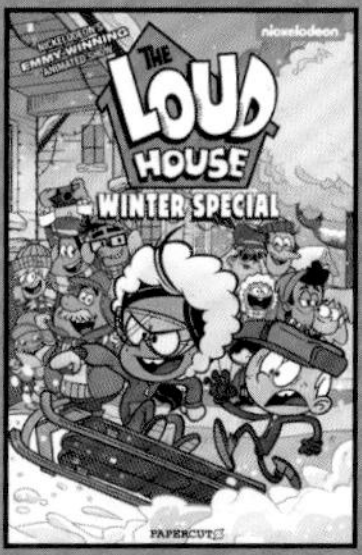

nickelodeon
THE LOUD HOUSE
WINTER SPECIAL
PAPERCUTZ

THE LOUD HOUSE
WINTER SPECIAL

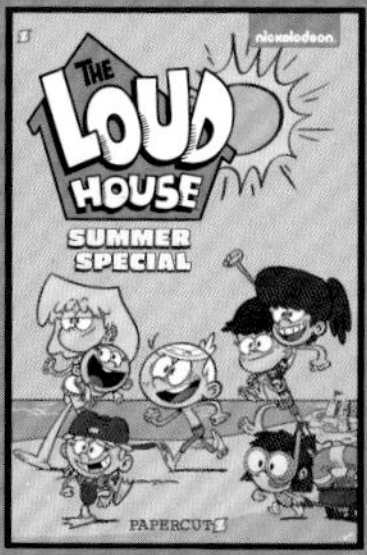

nickelodeon
THE LOUD HOUSE
SUMMER SPECIAL
PAPERCUTZ

THE LOUD HOUSE
SUMMER SPECIAL

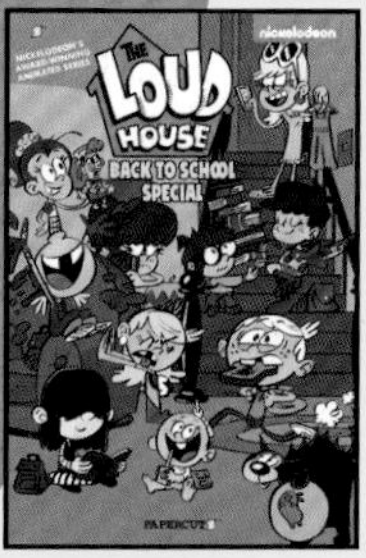

nickelodeon
THE LOUD HOUSE
BACK TO SCHOOL SPECIAL

THE LOUD HOUSE
BACK TO SCHOOL
SPECIAL

THE LOUD HOUSE and THE CASAGRANDES graphic novels and specials are available for $7.99 each in paperback, $12.99 each in hardcover. THE LOUD HOUSE 3 IN 1 and THE CASAGRANDES 3 IN 1 graphic novels are available for $14.99 each in paperback only.

Available from booksellers everywhere. You can also order online from Papercutz.com, or call 1-800-886-1223, Monday through Friday, 9-5 EST. MC, Visa, and AmEx accepted. To order by mail, please add $5.00 for postage and handling for the first book ordered, $1.00 for each additional book and make check payable to NBM Publishing.
Send to: Papercutz, 160 Broadway, Suite 700, East Wing, New York, NY 10038.

Nickelodeon graphic novels are also available digitally wherever e-books are sold.

Exclusive preview of THE LOUD HOUSE #16 "Loud and Clear"...

"TAKEOUT FAUX PAS"

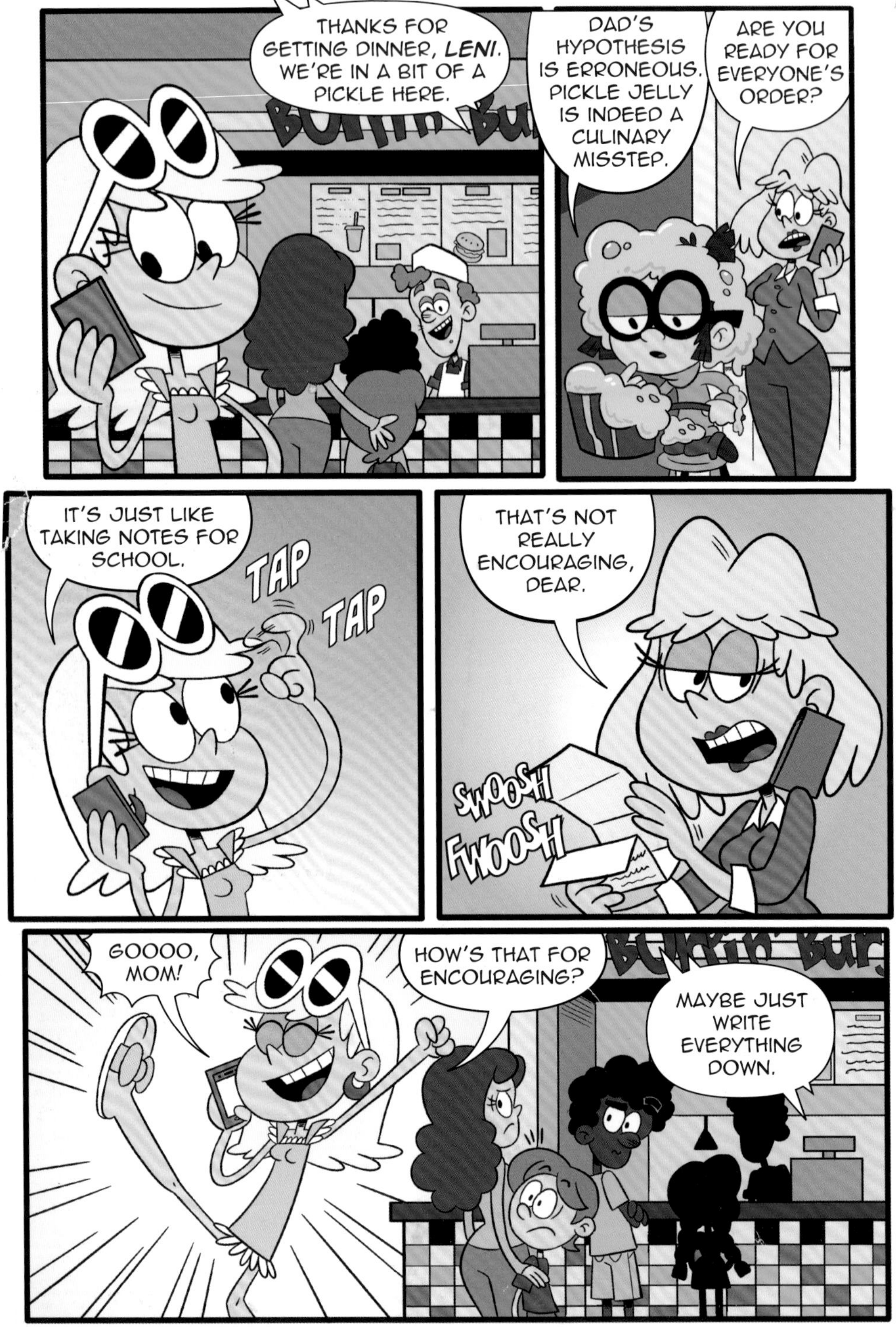
THANKS FOR GETTING DINNER, LENI. WE'RE IN A BIT OF A PICKLE HERE.
DAD'S HYPOTHESIS IS ERRONEOUS. PICKLE JELLY IS INDEED A CULINARY MISSTEP.
ARE YOU READY FOR EVERYONE'S ORDER?
IT'S JUST LIKE TAKING NOTES FOR SCHOOL.
TAP
TAP
THAT'S NOT REALLY ENCOURAGING, DEAR.
SWOOSH
FWOOSH
GOOOO, MOM!
HOW'S THAT FOR ENCOURAGING?
MAYBE JUST WRITE EVERYTHING DOWN.

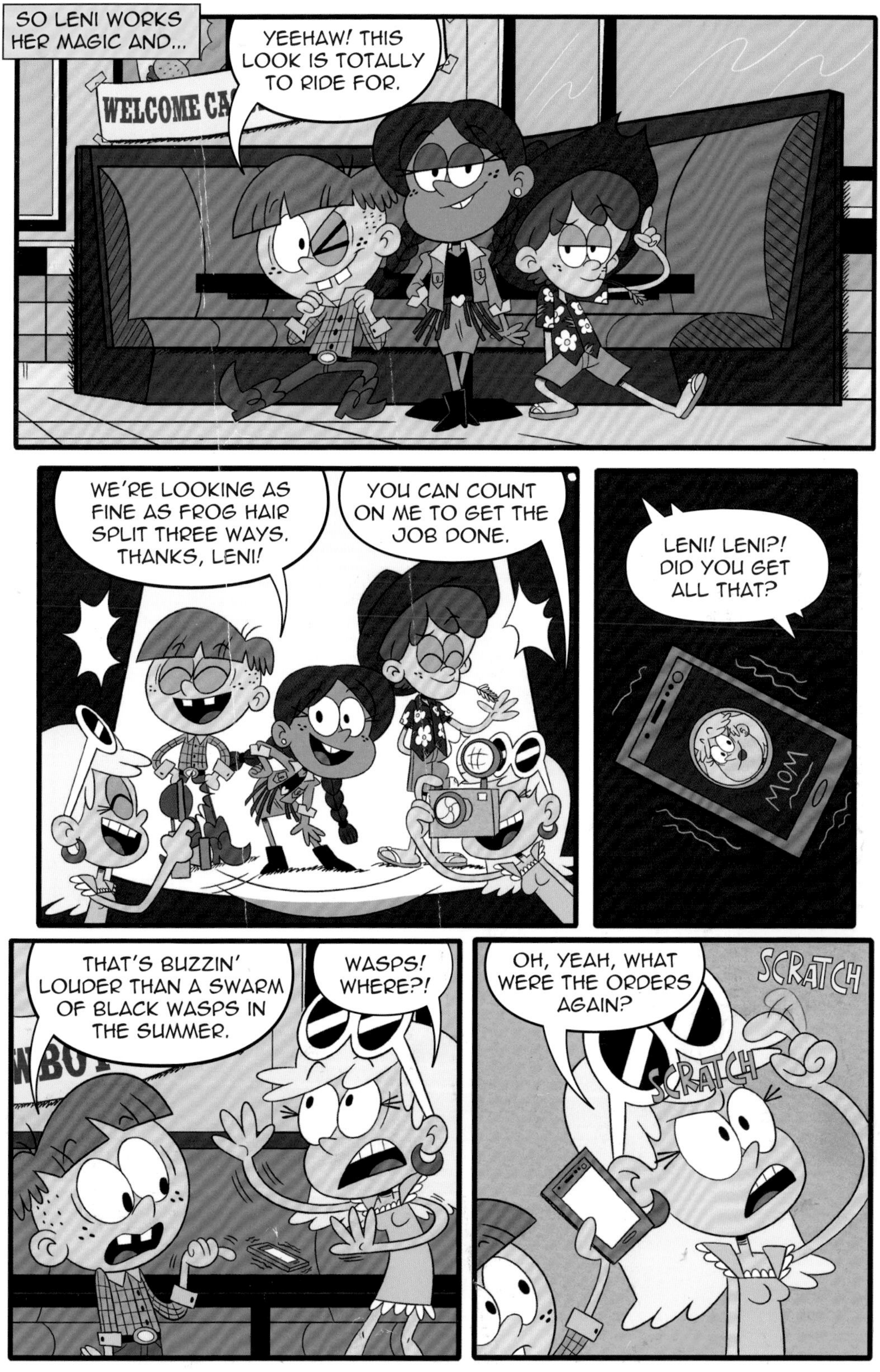
SO LENI WORKS HER MAGIC AND...
YEEHAW! THIS LOOK IS TOTALLY TO RIDE FOR.
WELCOME CA
WE'RE LOOKING AS FINE AS FROG HAIR SPLIT THREE WAYS. THANKS, LENI!
YOU CAN COUNT ON ME TO GET THE JOB DONE.
LENI! LENI?! DID YOU GET ALL THAT?
MOM
THAT'S BUZZIN' LOUDER THAN A SWARM OF BLACK WASPS IN THE SUMMER.
WASPS! WHERE?!
OH, YEAH, WHAT WERE THE ORDERS AGAIN?
SCRATCH
SCRATCH

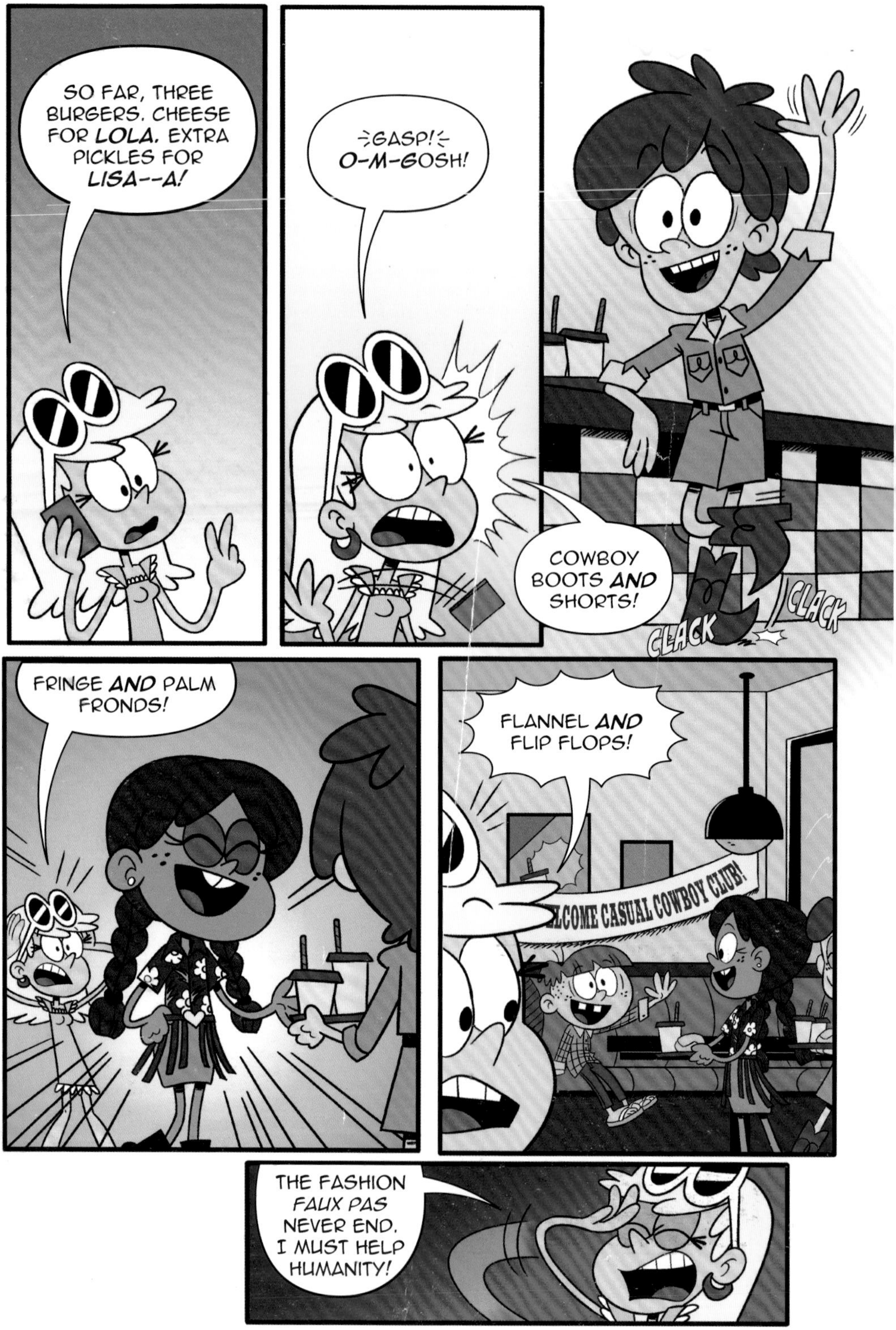
SO FAR, THREE BURGERS. CHEESE FOR LOLA. EXTRA PICKLES FOR LISA--A!
GASP! O-M-GOSH!
COWBOY BOOTS AND SHORTS!
CLACK
CLACK
FRINGE AND PALM FRONDS!
FLANNEL AND FLIP FLOPS!
LCOME CASUAL COWBOY CLUB!
THE FASHION FAUX PAS NEVER END. I MUST HELP HUMANITY!

To be continued in THE LOUD HOUSE #16!

Mariah Wilson—Writer • Jen Hernandez — Artist/Colorist • Wilson Ramos Jr — Letterer

THE LOUD HOUSE #16 "Loud and Clear" is coming soon to booksellers and libraries everywhere!